P9-CEJ-779

Papel Picado Art by Jenna Huerta

Design by Winnie Ho and Susan Gerber

Printed in the United States of America
First Hardcover Edition, October 2017
10 9 8 7 6 5 4 3 2 1
FAC-008598-17237
Library of Congress Control Number: 2017936309
ISBN 978-1-4847-8745-8

Visit disneybooks.com

SUSTAINABLE FORESTRY INITIATIVE Certified Sourcing
www.sfiprogram.org
SFI-00993
Logo Applies to Text Stock Only

DISNEY · PIXAR

COCO

A STORY ABOUT MUSIC SHOES, AND FAMILY

Adapted by
Diana López

DISNEY PRESS
Los Angeles • New York

Rivera

Tío Felipe   Tío Oscar

Tía Rosita   Papá Julio

Tía Victoria

Tía Carmen —— Tío Berto   Tía Gloria

Abel   Rosa   Benny   Manny

FAMILY TREE

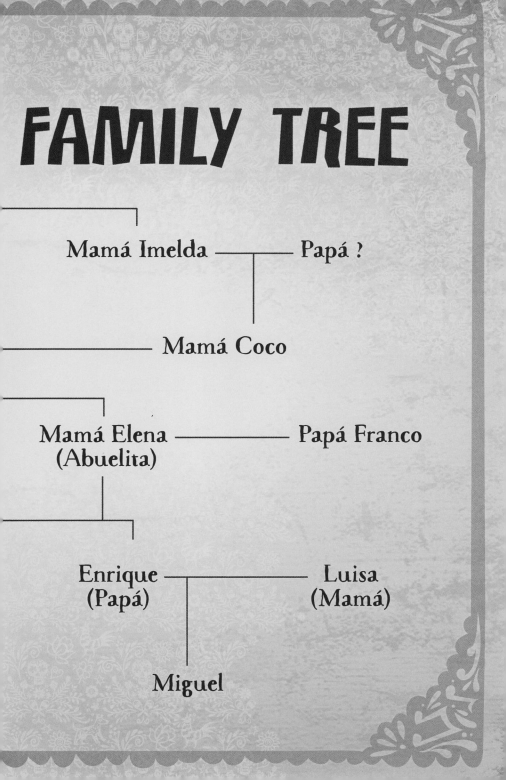

Mamá Imelda ——— Papá ?

Mamá Coco

Mamá Elena ——————— Papá Franco
(Abuelita)

Enrique ——————— Luisa
(Papá)   (Mamá)

Miguel

CHAPTER 1

Mamá Coco is the only person who truly understands Miguel. That's why he loves spending time with her.

"Hola, Mamá Coco," he says as he steps into his great-grandmother's room.

She's in a wicker wheelchair with her shawl and furry slippers. Her skin is as wrinkled as a wadded paper bag and her face is framed by two white trenzas, braids.

"How are you, Julio?" she says. Mamá Coco is very old, and sometimes she gets confused.

"Actually, my name is Miguel." He leans forward so she can get a good look at him. She lost her teeth long ago, but that doesn't stop her from smiling. "Heh, heh," she chuckles as she reaches for his cheeks.

Miguel tells her everything—how he likes to run with his hands open and palms flat because it's faster; how he has a dimple on one side of his face but not on the other; who his favorite luchador is. Mamá Coco nods and smiles, while the scraggly cat at the window yawns and stretches.

When he runs out of things to say, Miguel starts humming absentmindedly as he straightens things around the room. He catches Mamá Coco's foot moving, but he can't tell if she's trying to tap the rhythm or scratching an itch on her heel.

Without realizing it, Miguel stops humming and starts to sing out loud. He can't help it. The music just takes over.

He's about to hit a high note when his abuelita storms in.

"How many times do I have to tell you?" she says, pointing at him. "No music!"

She startles the cat at the window, and it runs off. She startles Mamá Coco and Miguel, too. Noticing this, Abuelita softens a bit and comes over to give Mamá Coco, her mother, a kiss on the forehead.

"Sorry I yelled," she says, and turning to Miguel, she adds, "but you know the rule—no music."

Miguel *does* know the rule. He's reminded every day. Once he blew into a glass soda bottle, and when Abuelita heard the whistle, she snatched the bottle away. Another time Miguel rushed to the window when he heard a truck with its radio blaring, but before he could catch the tune,

Abuelita angrily slammed the window shut. A few nights before, a trio of gentlemen had serenaded as they strolled by the family hacienda, and instead of letting them fill the air with beautiful songs, Abuelita burst out the door and chased them off. "No music!" she'd shouted after them.

And here she is again, telling him about the ban on music.

"I know the rule," Miguel says, "but—"

Abuelita shushes him. Then she sits on the edge of Mamá Coco's bed and pats the space beside her so Miguel can sit, too.

"Let me tell you why we have this rule," she begins. Miguel sighs. He's heard the story a million times. He can recite it by memory, and he says the words in his mind as Abuelita speaks. "A long time ago, there was a family. A mamá, a papá, and their little girl. The man, he was a musician. He loved to play the guitar while his wife and daughter danced. Every day, he and his wife would sing, dance, and count their blessings." Abuelita pauses and takes a deep breath before going on. "But this man had a dream. He wanted to play his music for the world. And one day, that man left with his guitar . . . and never returned." She shakes her head with shame, and her voice hardens a bit. "Now imagine a man holding a guitar and walking away as his poor wife and child stand in the doorway and watch. But do you think that woman wasted one tear on that walk-away musician? Tch—¡Claro que no!"

Miguel decides to finish the story. "She banished all music from her life because she had a daughter to provide for," he says, and Abuelita nods. "So she rolled up her sleeves and she learned to make shoes. Then she taught her daughter to make shoes. And later, she taught her son-in-law. Then her grandkids got roped in. As the business grew, so did her family."

Abuelita puts a hand on Miguel's shoulder. "And who was that woman?"

"My great-great-grandmother, Mamá Imelda."

"And the little girl?"

"Mamá Coco," Miguel answers, glancing at his great-grandmother as she sits in the wheelchair, nearly asleep.

Abuelita gets up and adjusts the shawl on Mamá Coco's shoulders. She beckons Miguel to follow her, and they tiptoe out, making their way to the ofrenda room. It's set up as a memorial to their ancestors, with an altar decorated with embroidered cloth, flowers, and candles illuminating portraits of relatives who have passed away. In the flickering light, the portraits seem to move as if the ancestors were still alive. Abuelita lovingly adjusts a sepia-tinted photo of Mamá Imelda with baby Coco on her lap. A man stands beside her, but his face has been torn away. The only clue that this is the mysterious musician is a charro jacket with fancy trim, the kind that mariachis love to wear.

"Come along," Abuelita says, and she leads Miguel across the courtyard to the shoemaking shop. Cabinets along the walls hold trays of buckles, shoelaces, brackets, threads, and chisels. Half-finished shoes hang from clotheslines, and different-sized mallets are thrown about. The floor is scuffed from so many years of the Rivera family hard at work. Even now, they are busy making shoes. Miguel's papá and tía Gloria use rivet guns to make eyelets for shoelaces. His mother and grandfather run fabric through sewing machines. Tío Berto carves into leather with a swivel knife, and Tía Carmen traces patterns on a cutting board. It's very noisy in the shop, but the tapping, punching, and sewing sound nothing like music to Miguel.

Abuelita waves her hand across the room as if showing Miguel a grand kingdom. "Music tore our family apart, but shoes have held it together." Then she giggles to herself. "In fact," she says, "I captured the heart of your grandfather when he realized that I made the most beautiful and comfortable cowboy boots in all of Mexico."

"I never got blisters," Papá Franco says.

"*No one* gets blisters when they wear *my* shoes," Abuelita proudly announces.

"Okay, okay," Miguel says. "Shoes. I get it." He slips a red hoodie over his tank top, grabs a shoeshine box, and heads for the door. "Why don't I make myself useful and go shine some boots in town?"

"Be back by lunch, m'ijo," his mamá says.

"And don't forget to use the brush on suede and the cloth on leather," Abuelita reminds him.

"Got it!" Miguel says, rushing to shine shoes like a proper Rivera boy. But, and this is the part he's left out, he plans to shine shoes near the musicians in Mariachi Plaza!

CHAPTER 2

On his way to the plaza, Miguel says hello to a woman who is whistling as she sweeps her stoop. Then he passes a lone guitarist playing a classical piece with lots of tremolo. Miguel nods with appreciation, and the man nods back. The closer Miguel gets to the plaza, the more music he hears and the happier he feels. Young girls sing while jumping rope, the slap on the sidewalk setting the tempo for their song. The church bells chime in harmony with a tune played by a street band, and when a radio blares a cumbia rhythm, Miguel does a few crossover steps to the beat.

He's humming when he reaches a pan dulce booth and

grabs his favorite type of sweet bread, the cochinito, a ginger-bread cookie shaped like a pig.

"Muchas gracias!" Miguel says as he tosses the vendor a coin.

"De nada, Miguel!"

As he walks along, he feels something at his leg, and when he looks down, he sees the scraggly cat from Mamá Coco's window. It scurries off, then glances back to see if Miguel is following. *Where does that cat want me to go?* he wonders.

He shrugs and moves on to a street vendor at a booth full of alebrijes, colorful sculptures of fantastical creatures, like lizards with feathers, rabbits with horns, and giraffes with multicolored spots. Miguel stops a moment, tapping a rhythm on the table. He's about to take a bite of pan dulce when a familiar street dog sidles up. The dog is nearly bald, with a few hairs sticking out here and there like thorns on a nopal. He goofily licks his chops because he's hungry.

Miguel breaks off the rump of the cochinito and holds it over the dog's nose. "Want some of this?" he asks, laughing.

"Roo, roo!" the dog answers.

Miguel goes through the commands he has taught the dog. "Sit, roll over, shake." The dog performs each trick perfectly. Miguel finishes with his favorite, "Fist bump," and he laughs as the the dog laps his long tongue against his closed hand. "Good boy, Dante!"

Miguel drops the pan dulce, and Dante gobbles it up.

There's a sense of celebration in the air because it's the eve of Día de los Muertos, the Day of the Dead, when the community honors loved ones who have passed away. The streets are lined with strings of papel picado, squares of paper with punched-out designs, brightening the space with their pinks, greens, golds, and blues. Children reach for decorated sugar skulls. Some of the elderly, viejitos and viejitas, carry candles and vases filled with marigolds and mums for their ofrendas, while others rush to buy soda, candy, fruit, cigars, or toys to leave at the gravesites.

Meanwhile, Miguel quickly makes his way to Mariachi Plaza with Dante at his side. They finally reach their destination, and the plaza lives up to its name, for it is crowded with musicians. *They're so lucky,* thinks Miguel, *to play guitars and trumpets without getting scolded.*

"I know I'm not supposed to like music," Miguel tells Dante, "but it's not my fault!" Miguel looks up and gazes at a statue of a handsome mariachi. "It's *his*: Ernesto de la Cruz, the greatest musician of all time." At the base of the statue is a plaque with the musician's most famous quote—SEIZE YOUR MOMENT.

Just then a tour group makes its way to the statue, and Miguel eavesdrops as the tour guide tells them about the famous musician.

"And right here in this very plaza," the tour guide says, "the young Ernesto de la Cruz took his first steps toward becoming the most beloved singer in Mexican history."

As the guide speaks, Miguel imagines de la Cruz in his heyday, a young man in the plaza, swarmed by fans as he played his songs.

He glances down at Dante and pets him. "De la Cruz," Miguel says, "he was just . . . he was the guy, you know? He started out a total nobody from Santa Cecilia, like me. But when he played music, he made people fall in love with him." Dante wags his tail. Miguel's told this story a dozen times, and Dante always seems happy to hear it. "He traveled the world," Miguel goes on. "He starred in movies. Oh, plus he had the coolest guitar. And he wrote the best songs! But my all-time favorite? It's—"

Miguel closes his eyes and recalls an old clip of de la Cruz performing in a fancy nightclub. He can clearly hear de la Cruz's voice singing his most famous song, "Remember Me." It's a song about being remembered forever—even after one is gone. And it has a very catchy tune.

Miguel hums along with the memory. Then he looks up at the statue of Ernesto de la Cruz, awestruck by his greatness.

"He lived the kind of life you dream about," he continues, "until 1942 . . ." He can't finish the sentence, because it breaks his heart to repeat what happened, but then he hears Dante panting and sees the goofy dog waiting for the end of the story. "Until 1942, when he was crushed by a giant bell."

Dante barks as if to say "the end." Then he runs off, and Miguel remembers why he's in the plaza. He's supposed to shine shoes, so he finds a spot near the statue and takes out his shoeshine kit, using the box as a footstool for his customers. A few minutes later, a mariachi asks for a shoeshine and Miguel gets to work, the whole time repeating the tale of Ernesto de la Cruz. "Sometimes, I look at de la Cruz," he says, "and I get this feeling . . . like we're connected somehow. Like, if *he* could play music, maybe someday I could, too." Then, in a voice full of sadness, he continues, "If only it wasn't for my family."

"Ay yai yai, muchacho!" the mariachi exclaims.

"Huh?" Miguel says, confused, because for a moment, he's forgotten where he is.

"I asked for a shoeshine, not your life story," the mariachi says.

"Oh, yeah. Sorry."

Miguel goes back to buffing the man's shoe. Meanwhile, the mariachi plucks at his guitar strings.

"I just can't talk about any of this at home," Miguel explains.

"Look," the mariachi says, "if I were you? I'd march right up to my family and say, 'Hey! I'm a musician. Deal with it.'"

Miguel shakes his head. "I could never say that."

"You *are* a musician, no?"

Miguel desperately wants to say yes, but then he remembers his family's past, how music tore them apart.

"I don't know," he admits. "I mean . . . I only really play for myself—"

"Aah!" The mariachi seems frustrated by Miguel's lack of confidence. "Did de la Cruz become the world's best musician by hiding his sweet, sweet skills?" He doesn't let Miguel answer. "No!" the mariachi says, thumping his guitar for emphasis. "He walked out onto that plaza and he played out loud!" He points to the gazebo, where some men are setting up speakers and hanging a giant poster announcing a talent show. "Ah! ¡Mira, mira! They're setting up for tonight. The music competition for Día de los Muertos. You wanna be like your hero? You should sign up!"

Instead of excited, Miguel is shocked at the thought. "Huh-uh, my family would freak!"

"Look, if you're too scared, then, well . . . have fun making shoes." The mariachi does a quick rasgueado on the guitar, and Miguel admires the way his fingers flutter over the strings. "But the world belongs to the bold, m'ijo." Miguel silently mouths the words as he considers this. "C'mon," the mariachi urges. "What did de la Cruz always say?"

"Seize your moment?" Miguel phrases it as a question even though he knows the answer by heart.

The mariachi nods. Then he offers the guitar to Miguel. "Show me what you got, muchacho. I'll be your first audience."

Miguel's eyes widen and his brows rise with surprise at this gesture. He aches to hold the guitar, but then he hears Abuelita proclaiming the family rule—*No music allowed!* Every time he dares to play something, her warning echoes in his head. But how can he resist a chance to touch a beautiful guitar?

He glances around to make sure the coast is clear. Then he reaches for the instrument and takes it with reverence, as if holding a holy relic. Once it's in his arms, Miguel presses the strings and is about to strum a C chord when he hears: "Miguel!"

It's Abuelita's voice, and he laughs at himself. *I must be paranoid*, he thinks. But then he hears her voice again, this time much closer. He gasps and tosses the guitar back to the mariachi, but it's too late. Abuelita, Tío Berto, and Prima Rosa, Miguel's cousin, have found them. They march straight over, their arms full of bags and supplies.

"Abuelita!" Miguel says.

"What are you doing here?" she asks.

"Um . . . uh . . ." Miguel quickly packs up his shoeshine equipment, hoping his grandmother ignores the mariachi.

But she doesn't. She grabs a chancla from her purse. Many years ago, the strap on the sandal fell off, but since Abuelita hates to throw out shoes, no matter how tattered, she keeps it as a flyswatter. Apparently, it's a mariachi swatter, too, because she barrels up to the man, hits him with the shoe, and waves him away just like she does with the flies.

"You leave my grandson alone!" she shouts.

"Doña, please. I was just getting a shine!"

"I know your tricks, mariachi!" Then, turning to Miguel, she demands, "What did he say to you?"

Miguel shrugs. "He was just showing me his guitar."

Abuelita gasps, Prima Rosa gasps, and Tío Berto gasps, too. "Shame on you!" the uncle says to the mariachi.

Abuelita approaches the musician, chancla aimed directly between his eyes. "My grandson," she says, "is a sweet little angelito querido cielito. He wants no part of your music, mariachi! You keep away from him!"

She is a formidable woman, so the mariachi grabs his

sombrero and scrambles away. Miguel can only watch with unspoken apologies and a heavy heart. There goes a man who let him talk about music without feeling ashamed.

"¡Ay, pobrecito!" Abuelita says, hugging Miguel so tight he can barely breathe. "¿Estás bien, m'ijo?" When she releases him, he gasps for air. "You know better than to be in this place! You will come home. *Now*."

Miguel sighs, and as he picks up his shoeshine box, he notices a sheet of paper. It's a flyer for the talent show—the one the mariachi told him about! Quickly, before Abuelita turns around, he pockets the flyer.

As they walk through the plaza, Abuelita can't stop commenting on everyone's shoes. When she sees Señor Maldonado, she says, "Now there is an admirable man. See how the patent leather of his loafers gleams in the sun?" When she sees Señora Diaz, she says, "I dyed those satin pumps myself, and look how they're fading." And to the señora, she calls out, "Don't store your shoes by the window! They're supposed to be red but now they're turning pink from all that sun." Señora Diaz gives her a thumbs-up and hurries away.

And then Rosa spots a small boy and points at him. "Look, Abuelita!"

Abuelita gasps. "His shoelaces!" Sure enough, the laces on the boy's tennis shoes are frayed and too short to be tied into a proper knot.

"Not his shoes," Rosa says. "He's *crying*!"

"Of course he's crying. I would cry, too, if my shoelaces

looked like that." Abuelita stoops down to examine them. "What happened here?" she asks the boy, but instead of explaining what happened to his shoes, he says, "I'm lost."

Abuelita snaps to get Tío Berto's attention. "Go find his parents," she orders.

"Yes, yes, right away," Tío Berto says as he obediently rushes off.

"We'll find your parents," Abuelita tells the boy. "In the meantime, you can't go around with frayed laces. Lucky for you, I have extras in my purse." She pulls out three pairs of shoelaces, and the boy's eyes widen with delight. "Which color do you want?" she asks, and he studies them as if choosing the right color is the most important decision of his life.

While Abuelita is busy with the boy, Miguel spots a paper airplane. It's crumpled from being stepped on. Thinking he can smooth out the crumpled parts and give it to the boy, Miguel picks it up, but he only half-heartedly unfolds it because he can't stop thinking about music. He really wants to perform. Except for Dante and Mamá Coco, no one's ever heard him sing. They don't *want* to hear him sing, because it's against the family rules. But what if he won the talent show? Maybe . . . just *maybe* they would accept him as a real musician.

He sighs, heavyhearted. Then he refolds the paper, making it a plane again, and throws it into the air. As it glides away, he thinks about his dreams. Will they glide away, too?

He's about to return to Abuelita when he hears clacking

from around the corner. He sneaks over to investigate, Rosa following. When they reach the sound, they find a group of ballet folklórico dancers.

"They're so pretty," Rosa says, admiring the full skirts with colorful petticoats and the hairstyles with ribbons and braids. The dancers are warming up for a performance, their toes and heels clacking on the sidewalk. "And they have the prettiest shoes," Rosa adds wistfully.

It's true. The shoes are very pretty, but Miguel is most interested in the metal plates on the heels and toes, because that is what makes the pleasant sound. He lifts a foot, examines the soles of his boots, and wonders if he could add his own metal plates. He's not allowed to play instruments, but maybe he could tap out rhythms with his feet.

"What are you doing?" Abuelita says, hands on hips.

Miguel lowers his foot. "We're just listening . . . I mean, *looking* at the dancers' beautiful shoes."

Abuelita has a skeptical expression on her face, but she lets it go. As they walk away, Miguel asks, "Abuelita, why don't we make *those* kinds of shoes, for the ballet folklórico dancers?"

When she doesn't answer, he asks again—and *again.*

"We just *don't!*" she says, and he knows better than to keep asking why.

CHAPTER 3

Many years ago, fifteen-year-old Coco hurried to the family's workshop with instructions from her mother to pick up five pairs of shoes and deliver them to the dancers in town. When she entered the shop, she found her uncles, Tío Oscar and Tío Felipe, side by side at their stations. They were identical twins, both wearing fedoras, long aprons, and striped shirts with the sleeves rolled up. Coco marveled at how their movements were perfectly matched as they pulled on needles with long lengths of thread.

"Hola, Coco," they said.

"What are you working on?" she asked.

"We're sewing tongues," Tío Oscar replied, and when he saw her surprise, he said, "Tongues for *shoes*, not the tongues you speak with."

"Or lick with," Tío Felipe added.

"Or whistle with."

"Or stick out when you're mad at your mamá Imelda."

Coco laughed. That was how her uncles talked, one after the other, and Coco had to pivot her head back and forth as she tried to keep up.

"Ay, tíos," she cried. "You're going to give me a headache!"

"Perdóname," both uncles said, and they immediately got back to sewing, pulling their needles in unison again. Coco hated to interrupt them, but she needed to pick up the shoes.

"Are the dancing shoes ready? Mamá said you made five pairs."

"Of course," Tío Felipe said. "One of us made three pairs—"

"And the other made two," finished Tío Oscar.

Coco followed them to the far corner of the shop, where they brought down two boxes from a shelf. As they pulled out shoes, they counted. "One, two . . ." said Tío Oscar. "Three, four . . ." said Tío Felipe. And together, they said, "Five."

They left the shoes in a pile and returned to their workstations. Coco wrapped each pair in tissue paper and carefully placed them in a basket so she could carry them to town. Meanwhile, her uncles were stroking their pencil-thin mustaches as they tried to solve a riddle.

"Which needle is mine?" Tío Felipe said.

"And which is *mine*?" asked Tío Oscar.

"Well, I was using black thread."

"So was I. Perhaps we should measure."

They grabbed a measuring tape. "Same length!" they exclaimed.

"Mira, hermano," Tío Oscar said, "no offense, but I prefer to use my own needle."

"As do I."

Coco knew this discussion would last all day, so she marched over, picked up the needles, and handed them out.

"This one is yours and this one is yours," she said.

"How can you tell?" they asked.

"Because they're clearly different."

The uncles examined the needles, doubtful expressions on their faces. "They *are*?"

"Yes!" Coco said, and pointing to each of her uncles, she continued, "As different as *you* and *you*!"

"Well, that makes perfect sense," Tío Oscar replied.

"It most certainly does," agreed Tío Felipe.

"We're as different as boots and sandals."

"As buckles and laces."

"As heels and flats."

"As . . ."

Coco grabbed her basket of shoes and rushed out before she got another headache. She loved her uncles, but they sure knew how to confuse her sometimes.

Coco enjoyed the bright sunshine as she headed to the dance studio. It was a quiet walk, and she heard only her steps and the rustle of her skirt. But once she reached the center of town, more sounds layered in—children laughing on the playground, vendors calling out their wares, and dogs barking for treats.

She crossed the plaza, turned a corner, and found the studio. "Anybody here?" she called, because it was empty when she stepped in.

"We're in the back," someone answered.

She followed the voice to a dressing room, where a seamstress was taking measurements of the girls. When they saw Coco, they clapped in delight, because her family had already earned a reputation for making excellent shoes.

As soon as she set down the basket, the girls rushed to it, unwrapped the shoes, and tried them on. Then one of the girls ran to the studio and started skipping around, a simple version of the polka. Soon all five girls joined her, their footsteps rhythmically clacking and echoing one another. There wasn't a single instrument in the room, yet it seemed filled with music.

Watching them reminded Coco of a time when *she* used to dance, too. She had been very young when her father left, so she couldn't remember his face very well, but she *could* remember his voice and the joy she had felt as she'd danced with her mother whenever he'd played the guitar and sung.

"Look!" the dance teacher said, disrupting Coco's memory. "Here's an extra pair of shoes."

Coco peeked into the basket and realized her uncles' mistake. Each had made three pairs, so instead of five, there were *six* pairs of shoes. Coco laughed to herself. Leave it to them to copy each other exactly.

For a moment, she thought about giving the extra shoes to the dancers in case another girl joined their group, but then she had a better idea. She would keep them for herself!

She finished the transaction, rushed home, and went behind the family compound to try the shoes. They fit perfectly! She did a little hop, then another and another. On the hard-packed dirt, her steps landed with a soft thud. She tiptoed to the paved patio, stepped onto the bricks, and heard the pleasant clicking of her shoes. She did a toe tap, cautiously, as if testing the temperature of a pool before jumping in. Then she glanced about. No one was around, so she decided it was safe to dance. Her first steps were a bit awkward because she hadn't danced in such a long time, but she was a natural. She felt rhythm in her blood. She didn't need musicians to sing, because she had the memory of her father's voice. She closed her eyes and the dancing took her back to the happiest memories of her early childhood. Soon she was flicking her feet, striking the ground with her toes and heels, and twirling her skirt. Her steps were getting faster, more rhythmic, and louder. Her footsteps echoed off the walls, and Coco imagined a dozen dancers celebrating beside her!

Then she heard someone's voice: "Ahem!"

Coco froze and opened her eyes. There stood Mamá Imelda, clearing her throat to get Coco's attention. She cradled a kitten and absently scratched behind its ears, making the little cat purr. Coco wondered how her mother's arms could be so tender when her eyes could be so stern.

"Um . . . uh . . . hola, Mamá."

"I thought I told you to deliver those shoes."

"I did," Coco said, "but there was an extra pair, so I thought . . . well, I wanted . . . and . . ."

Her mother raised an eyebrow, questioning, and Coco hung her head, ashamed. Then Mamá Imelda set down the kitten, approached her daughter, and lifted Coco's chin. This time her eyes were as gentle as her hands.

"M'ija," she said, "look around." Mamá Imelda stood back and looked at the hacienda with appreciation. "We have a comfortable home, delicious food, and warm clothes, but more importantly, we have each other, and all because we know the difference between good, honest work and . . . careless indulgences."

Coco nodded. "I understand, but—"

"It's very simple," Mamá Imelda interrupted. "Music tore our family apart, but shoes have kept us together." She straightened Coco's braids. "From now on," she said, "the dancers can order from someone else. These shoes bring too many sad memories, and some things are better to forget." Then she headed to the workshop, the kitten following close behind.

Disheartened, Coco headed to her room to take off the shoes. They still clicked as she stepped on the pavement, but instead of music, the clicks sounded like someone hammering shut her joy.

CHAPTER 4

Miguel trudges along with his family. He's carrying his shoeshine box and an armful of marigolds. He's still getting lectured, even though they're halfway home now.

"How many times have we told you?" Tío Berto says. "That place is crawling with mariachis!"

"Yes, Tío Berto."

Prima Rosa gives him a sympathetic look, but she doesn't jump to his defense. Miguel can't blame her. If she takes his side, she'll get in trouble, too.

Then Dante ambles up, sniffs the bags Miguel's relatives are carrying, and whines for treats.

"No, no, no, no, no," Miguel says to the hairless dog,

because he knows what's going to happen next—and sure enough, it does.

"Go away, you! Go!" Abuelita says, throwing the chancla at Dante. It works. The frightened dog runs off.

"It's just Dante," Miguel explains.

"Never name a street dog," Abuelita warns. "It'll follow you forever. Now, go get my shoe!"

Miguel stoops to pick it up. It's tricky since he's holding so many things, but he manages to grab the shoe and secure it under his arm. His family has finally stopped scolding him, but Miguel knows it won't last. Lectures usually aren't over until everyone has chimed in, and with a family as big as his, that's a lot of people.

Then he spots another talent show flyer, this one nailed to a post. His family is walking ahead, their backs to him. He can hear their voices talking about Día de los Muertos, and from the opposite direction, he can hear the faint sounds of music. He leans toward it. The music *calls* him. He feels torn between his devotion to family and his desire for music. There has to be a way to get the best of both worlds. What if he . . . yes! He pats the flyer in his pocket, making sure it's still there. He will enter the contest, but he'll keep it a secret. That way, he can be a musician *and* keep his family happy.

As soon as they get to the family compound, Abuelita marches them to the shoemaking shop. Everyone is busy at work, including his teenaged primo, Abel, who's guiding shoes through an automated polisher. Miguel knows the drill. He sets down his supplies, plops on a stool, and braces himself for more lecturing.

Abuelita grabs two wooden shoe stretchers, using them as clappers to get everyone's attention. "I found your son in Mariachi Plaza!" she tells Miguel's parents.

"Miguel . . ." Papá says, disappointed, and Mamá says, "You know how Abuelita feels about the plaza."

"I was just shining shoes!"

"A *musician's* shoes!" Tío Berto reveals.

Everyone gasps, including Abel, causing his shoe to zip away from the polisher and fly up to the roof. A few seconds later, it falls and bops him on the head.

"But the plaza's where all the foot traffic is," Miguel explains.

"If Abuelita says no more plaza," Papá says, "then no more plaza."

"But what about tonight?" Miguel asks.

"What's tonight?" Papá Franco wants to know.

Miguel hesitates before speaking, but he can't help spilling his secret. "It's Día de los Muertos. The whole town's gonna be there and . . . well . . . they're having this talent show."

Abuelita narrows her eyes and crosses her arms. "*Talent* show?"

Miguel gulps and squirms in his seat. "And I thought I might . . ."

"Sign up?" Mamá guesses.

"Well, maybe?"

Prima Rosa laughs. "You have to have *talent* to be in a talent show."

"Yeah," Abel adds. "What are you going to do, shine shoes?"

Miguel hates it when his primos tease him. Why can't they take *his* side once in a while?

"I *do* have a talent," Miguel insists, "but . . . it's . . ." He spots the quizzical expressions on his parents' faces. "Well, it's . . . it's a surprise."

"Absolutely not!" Abuelita says. "It's Día de los Muertos, and no one's going anywhere. Tonight is about family." She grabs the marigolds that Miguel set down and the ones Rosa had carried, and she gives them to him. There are so many petals that Miguel nearly inhales a few and has to spit them out. "Ofrenda room," Abuelita orders. "¡Vámonos!"

Miguel follows Abuelita to the ofrenda room, and when they enter, they see that Mamá Coco is already there. Miguel smiles at her, but before he can say hello, Abuelita orders him to hold the flowers while she arranges them on the altar. He wishes he could be alone with Mamá Coco and tell her about the talent show. *She would understand, unlike* . . . He glances at his grandmother.

"Don't give me that look," Abuelita says. "It's the one night of the year our ancestors can come visit us." She takes a moment to adjust the flower arrangement. "We've put their photos on the ofrenda so their spirits can cross over. We made all this food, and set out the things they loved in life, m'ijo."

Every year, Abuelita stresses this important tradition.

Only the spirits with pictures on an ofrenda can enjoy the offerings left in the home and at the gravesites. The pictures are like boarding passes, and without them, the spirits remain stuck on the other side.

While she's preoccupied with the flowers, Miguel takes a few steps toward the door. He needs to practice. The talent show is only a few hours away.

"All this work to bring the family together," Abuelita says, "so I don't want you sneaking off to who-knows-where."

She reaches for a flower, but Miguel's not there. He's halfway to the door.

"Where are you going?" she demands.

"I thought we were done."

"Ay, Dios mío," she sighs, exasperated. "Being part of this family means being *here* for this family. I don't want to see you end up like—" She glances at the photo of young Mamá Coco, her mother, Imelda, and the faceless musician.

"Like Mamá Coco's papá?"

"Never mention that man!" Abuelita says. "He's better off forgotten."

"But you're the one who—"

"Ta, ta, ta-tch!" Abuelita will not let him speak.

Miguel's about to push the issue, but then they hear Mamá Coco's gravelly voice. "Papá? Papá is home?"

Abuelita rushes to her. "Mamá, cálmese, cálmese."

"Papá is coming home?" Mamá Coco asks again.

"No, Mamá. But it's okay. I'm here."

With Abuelita preoccupied, Miguel sneaks away. He

doesn't hear Mamá Coco ask his abuelita, "Who are you?" He doesn't see the sadness on his grandmother's face as she tells Mamá Coco to rest while she gently pats the old lady's hands. He doesn't hear Abuelita try to tell him, "I'm hard on you because I care," and he also fails to hear her sigh when she realizes that he's gone.

Miguel can only shake his head as he passes Tío Berto and his papá unloading rolls of leather from a truck. The sun is bright, so he must squint as he makes his way through the family compound. When he reaches a giant cypress tree, he looks around to make sure no one's watching. Then he climbs the tree onto the roof, carefully scuttles across the tiles, lifts a sign advertising the family business, and slips into the space behind it. This is Miguel's secret attic hideout, the one place where he can get away from his family's expectations and just be himself.

In a corner are several pairs of shoes that someone discarded years ago. Miguel ignores them and focuses on an ofrenda he built to honor the memory of Ernesto de la Cruz. He lights a few candles to illuminate the posters, songbooks, and albums that he has carefully arranged. But the candles reveal something else, too—a guitar! It's not as fancy as the guitar that de la Cruz holds on his album covers or even as fancy as the guitar he held earlier in the plaza, but it's just as special, because Miguel has crafted this instrument himself. He cobbled it from scraps he found in Mariachi Plaza and around the shoemaking shop—a beat-up soundboard, old strings, a bridge made from a comb, and tuning pegs made from bent nails. The instrument is held together with duct tape, leather scraps, and lots of love. Studying one of Ernesto de la Cruz's album covers, Miguel takes a marker and traces the one-of-a kind skull designs from the famous musician's guitar. Miguel's version is slightly off-center and a bit crude, but he decides it's good enough.

He's about to tune the guitar when he hears footsteps pattering on the roof and the sign moving. Someone has discovered his hideout in the attic! Miguel gasps, but before he can blow out the candles, Dante peeks in.

"Oh, it's you," Miguel says, relieved. "Get in here. C'mon, Dante. Hurry up."

The dog wriggles in and sniffs the entire periphery of the room, spending an unusually long time on the shoes in the corner. Then he plops in front of Miguel, an attentive audience.

"I just . . . I just wish I could get someone to listen," Miguel says as he tunes the guitar. "Other than you," he tells Dante, who replies by sloppily licking Miguel's face. Miguel gives a grossed-out chuckle and turns his attention back to the guitar, strumming a chord that vibrates off the walls. "¡Perfecto!"

He studies the album cover. Ernesto de la Cruz poses confidently with his beaming white smile, and Miguel imitates him. He's a little awkward, but pretending to be de la Cruz for a moment makes him feel better.

Then he picks up a videotape with *Best of de la Cruz* scrawled on the label. He turns on an old TV set and pushes the tape into a VCR. Like the guitar, Miguel made the tape himself, a montage of his favorite scenes from de la Cruz's movies and interviews.

The first scenes come from a movie called *A quien yo amo.* Miguel strums to provide some musical accompaniment as de la Cruz imparts his wisdom.

"I have to sing," de la Cruz says. "I have to play. The music, it's not just in me. It *is* me."

Miguel nods. This is exactly how he feels, too.

"When life gets me down," de la Cruz continues, "I play my guitar. The rest of the world may follow the rules, but I must follow my heart!" De la Cruz passionately kisses a woman, and Miguel cringes.

Then there's another clip from the film. In this one de la Cruz holds a guitar. "You know that feeling? Like there's a song in the air and it's playing just for you?" Ernesto de la Cruz pauses and begins to strum the guitar. Miguel mimics the hand positions so he can follow along as his idol begins to sing about never knowing he could want something so much.

After a few verses, the song ends, and the videotape switches to another movie called *Nuestra iglesia.* In this scene, de la Cruz plays a good-natured priest speaking to a nun.

"You must have faith, Sister!"

"Oh, but Padre, he will never listen."

"He will listen to *music*!" Now de la Cruz bursts into song. He sings about music, how it has the power to change minds and hearts. He goes on, and since Miguel knows all the words, he follows along. When the song ends, de la Cruz tells the nun, "Never underestimate the power of music."

The tape switches again, this time to a romantic scene with de la Cruz professing his love to a woman named Lola. She says, "But my father, he will never give his permission." And de la Cruz replies, "I am done asking permission. When you see your moment, you mustn't let it pass you by. You must seize it!"

Immediately after these famous lines is a clip of an interview. "Señor de la Cruz, what did it take for you to seize your moment?"

De la Cruz does not hesitate to answer. "I had to have faith in my dream. No one was going to hand it to me. It was up to me to reach for that dream, grab it tight, and make it come true."

"And make it come true," Miguel repeats.

The tape ends, but Miguel can still hear the words repeating in his mind. If he wants to be a musician, he'll have to make it happen. When he sees an opportunity, he must seize it, just like Ernesto de la Cruz.

He reaches into his pocket to pull out the talent show flyer. "No more hiding, Dante. I gotta seize my moment!"

Dante wags his tail and pants happily.

"I'm going to play in Mariachi Plaza if it kills me!"

CHAPTER 5

Miguel grabs his guitar and, for inspiration, his favorite album. Then he and Dante scurry out across the roof and peek over the edge. They must be stealthy in order to sneak away. Luckily, the setting sun casts long shadows, making it easier to hide—but then the courtyard fills up with people as Abuelita opens all the doors and announces, "Día de los Muertos has begun!"

Miguel hides on the roof as children run by with sparklers. Then he spots his twin primos, toddlers Manny and Benny, carrying baskets of marigold petals and haphazardly scattering them on the ground.

"No, no, no, no, no," Mamá corrects them. "We have to make a clear path." She demonstrates, creating a path from the ofrenda room to the front gate. "These petals guide our ancestors home. We don't want them to get lost. We want them to come and enjoy all the food and drinks on the ofrenda, ¿sí?"

The toddlers nod, their eyes full of wonder and anticipation. They follow Mamá. Miguel and Dante take the opportunity to drop from the roof, just outside the compound, but the coast isn't clear, because Papá and Tío Berto round the corner carrying a small table from storage.

"Where should we put this table?" Papá calls out.

Miguel and Dante back up toward the courtyard to avoid the adults, only to find Abuelita shaking out a rug. She's turning toward them! Luckily, Miguel and Dante jump into the ofrenda room before she sees them.

"In the courtyard, m'ijos," Abuelita answers. She is out of sight but her voice is clear.

"You want it down by the kitchen?"

"Sí. Eh . . . next to the other one."

Inside the ofrenda room, they find Mamá Coco, and Miguel puts his finger to his lips so she will keep his presence a secret. But it's too late. He hears Abuelita's voice—right outside the door!

"Miguel!"

"Hurry! Under the table," Miguel tells Dante as he stuffs his guitar and album beneath the tablecloth. "Get under! Get under!"

"Miguel!" Abuelita calls again.

"Nothing!" he says, panicked.

He whips around. Abuelita and his parents are looking at him. His heart is racing and his palms are sweaty from the stress of almost getting caught. He wants to pretend like nothing unusual is going on, but he can't help stammering. "Mamá . . . Papá . . . I . . ."

Papá lifts a finger to silence him. "Miguel." He takes a deep breath. "Your abuelita had the most wonderful idea!" He giggles with excitement. "We've all decided—it's time you joined us in the workshop!"

"What?!" Miguel says.

He's heard rumors about people seeing their lives pass before them when they have near-death experiences, and that's what happens to him. Miguel hears the announcement and immediately sees his visits to Mariachi Plaza, bands performing in the gazebo, his secret hideout where he plays guitar and watches film clips, Mamá Coco's room where he quietly hums. If he starts making shoes, he won't have time to do anything related to music. It breaks his heart to realize this. But how can he tell his family? He loves them and doesn't want to disappoint them, especially when their faces are beaming with pride because becoming an apprentice is a big step.

I think I'm cursed, Miguel decides, *because of something that happened before I was even born.*

Papá holds out an apron and drapes it over Miguel. The apron is made of leather, but for Miguel, it's heavier than the steel armor that the conquistadors wore. He feels trapped by it and by all the expectations it represents.

"No more shining shoes. You'll be *making* them!" Papá says proudly. "Every day after school."

"No more going into town?" Miguel's voice cracks, but no one seems to notice. They just stand there, still beaming with pride.

Abuelita grabs Miguel's cheeks and squeezes them affectionately. "Ooh! Our Miguelito's carrying on the family tradition. And on Día de los Muertos! Your ancestors will be so proud!" She gestures to the shoes adorning the ofrenda. "You'll craft huaraches just like your tía Victoria."

"And wingtips," Papá adds, "like your papá Julio."

Miguel backs away from the ofrenda. He desperately wants to escape. "But what if I'm no good at making shoes?" He won't say his next thought out loud, but the truth is he doesn't even *like* the idea of making shoes.

"Aw, Miguel," Papá says. "You have your family here to guide you." He waves his arm as if presenting the family. "You are a Rivera, and a Rivera is . . ."

"A shoemaker," Miguel finishes, his voice defeated. "A shoemaker through and through."

Everyone turns to admire the photos on the altar. Miguel peeks over their shoulders to see even *more* generations of his family, and he starts to feel claustrophobic in the tiny room crowded with Papá, Mamá, Abuelita, Mamá Coco, and too many ancestors to count.

"That's my boy! Ha-ha!" Papá says. Then he calls out, "Berto, break out the good stuff. I wanna make a toast!"

As Papá heads out of the room, Mamá gives Miguel a soft smile. He smiles back, trying his best to fake happiness. Satisfied, she follows Papá out the door. Last is Abuelita, who smothers Miguel with tons of kisses before exiting.

With the family gone, Miguel turns back to the ofrenda and discovers Dante on the table, chomping at the pan dulces they left for their ancestors. The bald dog has never looked more content, but Miguel is horrified.

"No, Dante! Stop!"

Miguel grabs the dog and pulls him away from the ofrenda, but all that movement shakes the table. The frame with Mamá Imelda's photo sways back and forth, and before Miguel can stop it, the picture topples to the ground with a sickening crack. The frame has broken, and Miguel must shake away the fragments as he lifts the picture. He knows Dante didn't mean it, but he feels like everyone is working against him. The last thing he needs is to get in trouble for breaking a picture.

"No, no, no, no, no!" Miguel cries.

He holds the old photo of Mamá Imelda with a young Coco and the mysterious headless musician. Suddenly, he notices that a section of the picture has been folded and hidden by the frame all these years. Miguel desperately wants to unfold it, but he hesitates because he feels like he's prying. The hidden section is like a locked door or a gate with a NO TRESSPASSING sign, but he can't help it. He has to look! When he unfolds the picture, he gasps. Next to the mysterious musician is a guitar—not just any guitar—but *the* guitar—the one with a skull carved into its head!

Miguel is beside himself. "De la Cruz's guitar?"

Then Mamá Coco speaks. "Papá?" she says, pointing at the picture. "Papá?"

Miguel's eyes widen as the connection dawns on him. Could it possibly be true? *But of course,* Miguel thinks. *I have always felt a great connection to this musician.* His father was right when he told Miguel to look to the family for guidance. The answer was there all along!

He grabs his record album from beneath the table and sets it beside the photo. The guitars are a perfect match! Miguel can't believe it. He has admired this guitar for as long as he can remember. The tuning pegs, the rosette, the bridge, the skull designs on its head and body . . . for Miguel, these details make the guitar more than just an instrument. They make it a work of art.

He kneels beside Mamá Coco's wheelchair and shows her the picture. "Mamá Coco, is this your papá—Ernesto de la Cruz?"

"Papá! Papá!" she replies.

It all makes sense. Mamá Imelda's husband left his family to seek fame and fortune. Ernesto de la Cruz indeed became a rich and famous musician who played a guitar that looked exactly like the guitar in the photo. What did he say in *A quien yo amo? "The music, it's not just in me. It is me."* Music runs in Miguel's blood, too—not just shoes. Órale, the headless musician standing beside Mamá Imelda must be Ernesto de la Cruz!

"'I am done asking permission,'" Miguel says, quoting one of his favorite movies, determination rising. "'When you see your moment, you mustn't let it pass you by. You must seize it!'"

Miguel will no longer keep his love for music a secret. He's tired of hiding and pretending. It's time the family learns the truth, the *real* truth. It's time they accept him for who he really is!

Miguel grabs the guitar and runs into the courtyard with his instrument, photo, and album. His entire family is related to the most famous musician in Mexico! Perhaps with this new information, they will finally understand.

"Papá! Papá!" he calls.

Everyone turns to look at him—his parents, his grandparents, his aunts, uncle, and primos.

"It's him!" Miguel says. "I know who my great-great-grandfather was!" He takes a deep breath before making his big announcement. "Mamá Coco's father was Ernesto de la Cruz!"

"What are you talking about?" Papá says.

Miguel sets down his items, whips off the cobbler's apron, and strikes the pose from de la Cruz's album. "I'm gonna be a musician!"

The family encircles him, and at that moment, Abuelita takes a good look at his handmade guitar. "What is all this? You keep secrets from your own family?"

"It's all that time he spends in the plaza," Tío Berto says.

"Fills his head with crazy fantasies," adds Tía Gloria.

"It's not a fantasy!" insists Miguel. He picks up the photo of the faceless musician, hands it to his father, and points at the guitar. "That man was Ernesto de la Cruz, the greatest musician of all time!"

Papá takes the photo, looks at it, and sighs heavily. "We've never known anything about this man. But whoever he was, he still abandoned his family. This is no future for my son."

"But Papá, you told me to look to the ofrenda. You said my family would guide me! Well, de la Cruz is my family! I'm supposed to play music!"

"Never!" Abuelita says. "That man's music was a curse! I will not allow it!"

"If you would just—"

"Miguel," Mamá warns, and Papá, in a stern voice, says, "You will listen to your family. No more music."

"Just listen to me play."

"End of argument," Papá says.

Once again, Miguel remembers de la Cruz's words about seizing your moment and fighting for what you want. He picks up his guitar, but before he strums a chord, Abuelita snatches it away. Then she points to the man in the photo.

"You want to end up like that man?" she asks angrily. "Forgotten? Left off your family's ofrenda?!"

"I don't care if I'm on some stupid ofrenda!"

The family gasps, and Abuelita's eyes harden. Miguel knows this is a direct insult to their way of life, to everything they believe in, but what about *his* way of life? *His* beliefs? Don't they matter, too?

He never gets a chance to explain, because Abuelita lifts the guitar, and guessing what she's about to do, Miguel shouts, "No!" and Papá shouts, "Mamá!"

But it's too late. Abuelita forcefully throws the guitar, smashing it to bits—the guitar neck like a broken bone, the strings like torn ropes. Miguel wants to wail but he's too shocked. He thinks about gathering parts for the guitar, putting it together, and playing it—all those hours of work and joy smashed in a matter of seconds.

"There. No guitar, no music," Abuelita says, victorious. "Come. You'll feel better after you eat with your family."

But Miguel's heart feels as smashed as his guitar, and no amount of food is going to make him feel better.

"I don't want to be in this family!"

He snatches the photo from his father and bolts out of the hacienda, Dante following.

"Miguel! Miguel!" Papá calls, but Miguel ignores him. He is the great-great-grandson of Ernesto de la Cruz, and he, too, will seize his moment—even if it means running away from his entire family.

CHAPTER 6

COCO, a young woman now, stood before her closet, deciding what to wear. She had many shoes—pumps, sandals, boots, and heels. Most were quite beautiful and very comfortable, but some were totally useless or odd because her uncles often tinkered with new designs. They once made cleaning shoes with thick bristles on the soles for scrubbing the floor while walking, but the bristles went flat as soon as the customers took their first steps. Another time they made boots with pockets for storing keys and money, but no one wanted to reach down to their shoes when reaching into their coats or purses was easier.

"You are not inventors. You are shoemakers," Mamá

Imelda told them, throwing away the bad designs. But Coco loved the shoes and the playful imagination they represented, so she rescued them for her collection. She smiled every time she saw her uncles' failed experiments, though she never wore them. She preferred to wear strappy heels because they showed off her painted toenails.

Coco grabbed a pair of heels and buckled them around her ankles. Then, after making sure her braids were tight and straight, she went to the courtyard and found her mother setting down a bowl for the cat.

"Mamá," Coco said, "I'm heading to town to pick up supplies for Oscar and Felipe."

Mamá Imelda smiled as the cat messily lapped the milk. "They must need a lot of supplies," she said. "You've been going to town almost every day."

"Uh . . . yes . . . haha," Coco chuckled nervously. "You know how they are—so disorganized."

Mamá Imelda nodded, but she had a doubtful expression on her face. "Very well. Since you're heading to town, can you also pick up some flour?"

"Of course," Coco said, kissing her mother on the cheek before rushing away.

As she walked into town, she felt a little guilty because she'd told a lie. It was true that her uncles often sent her for supplies, but sometimes, like today, Coco went to town for other reasons. *Secret* reasons. And if Mamá Imelda knew what she was up to, she'd probably lock Coco in a dungeon—because Coco went into town so she could dance!

Many young people danced as the bands played in Mariachi Plaza. At first, Coco would sit on a bench to watch as they circled the plaza. Then she'd get restless, so she'd practice on the sidelines, copying the steps and pretending to have her own partner—until one day, Julio, a young man with a dark mustache, asked her to dance. First he taught her the rapid one-two-three of polkas. Coco loved the festive accordions and the way her heart raced as she and Julio skipped along with the quick beat. Then he taught her the waltz, her favorite. It, too, had a one-two-three rhythm, but much slower. At first Coco kept stepping on Julio's feet, but eventually she learned to match his stride and to recognize the subtle pressure of his hands as he signaled her to twirl or change direction. Today they danced the polka *and* the waltz, and they would have danced all day if Coco hadn't spotted a flower cart passing by.

"I have to get flowers for my mother," she said. "She's waiting."

Julio nodded, and they went to the cart. Mamá Imelda hadn't specified what kind of flowers she wanted, so Coco selected a bushel of daisies. Meanwhile, Julio bought her a red rose.

"You deserve a flower, too," he said, making her blush. Coco tucked it in her hair, relishing its perfume as she walked home.

When she got there, she went to the kitchen, knowing it was time for Mamá Imelda to prepare dinner. "Here are the flowers," she said, handing over the daisies.

Mamá Imelda looked confused. "I meant flour for cooking, not *flowers*." Then she spotted the rose. "And where did you get that?" she asked, pointing.

Coco blushed again. "Oh . . . uh . . . *this*? The vendor was giving them away."

"Hmmm . . ." Mamá Imelda muttered. She seemed unconvinced, but she let it go. "Well, go fill a vase with water. Perhaps tomorrow you can pick up the *right* kind of flour."

"Yes, Mamá," Coco said, relieved.

The next day Coco returned to town, but before going to the grocer, she went to Mariachi Plaza for more dancing. Julio beamed when she arrived. The band played a cumbia, so they grabbed hands and danced side by side. Other couples danced, too, and Coco couldn't help laughing when she spotted a child holding both parents' hands and hopping up to swing from them. She *lived* for these moments and was having a wonderful time until she turned a corner and gasped! Right beside the gazebo was a cat—Mamá Imelda's cat—and it was staring straight at her!

She froze, and Julio asked what was wrong.

"My mother," Coco said, nodding toward Imelda, who was standing beside the cat with her arms crossed and her eyes glaring.

Coco approached, hanging her head with shame. "Hola, Mamá."

"I thought you seemed"—Mamá Imelda glanced at Julio—"distracted." She bent down and lifted the cat to her shoulder. "Luckily, my gato has excellent tracking skills. She found you right away." Then she turned to Julio and got right to business. "I'm Coco's mother, and you are . . . ?"

"Julio," he answered, nodding with respect.

"And your intentions with my daughter?"

"Only the most honorable," Julio answered quickly. He turned to Coco and looked at her directly. "I wish to marry her someday."

Coco's eyes widened and her heart raced, for this was how she felt about him, too.

But Mamá Imelda had a practical, rather than romantic, personality. "Do you have a trade?" she asked, listening carefully as Julio listed his skills. One in particular got her attention. "You can do upholstery?" she asked.

"Sí, señora. My abuelo has a shop."

She thought a minute. "If you can do upholstery, then surely you can make shoes."

"I have never tried," Julio answered, "but I'm a fast learner."

Mamá Imelda nodded and glanced back and forth from Coco to Julio. She seemed to be making a decision. Then her cat purred into her ear.

"Very well," she said. "Tomorrow you will come to the hacienda to meet the family and visit the shoemaking shop. And then, if you decide this is what you *truly* want, you can become our apprentice."

"I would appreciate the opportunity," Julio said.

"But there's one important rule," Mamá Imelda continued.

Julio nodded and ventured a guess. "Everyone says that

the Riveras are the finest shoemakers in town, but that they don't allow music."

"Yes," she said. "It brings us painful memories."

"It's because of my father," Coco explained with regret in her voice. "He loved music more than anything else."

"And he left us to pursue his dream," Mamá Imelda added. "We never heard from him again." She paused to let this sink in. "Music hurt this family, so we choose to live without it."

Julio seemed truly saddened by this, but then he said the magic words. "Family comes first. That's what I believe. And if your family has a rule against music, then I will honor it."

Later, as Coco headed home with her mother, her heart ached. On the one hand, she was glad that Julio accepted her family's conditions and placed love over selfish desires. On the other hand, she felt hurt that she'd never dance with him again.

"Can't we have music?" Coco asked her mother. "Not every day but *sometimes*? On special occasions?"

"Why would we want to ruin special occasions with painful memories?"

"But Mamá, it can't be as bad as we think. After all, music and dancing is how I met Julio."

"And shoes, m'ija, is how you will *stay* with him."

CHAPTER 7

Miguel sprints to town, Dante at his feet. He passes an overturned trash can, a bike with a flat tire, and a fallen tree. Everything seems as broken as he feels, everything except for a large poster announcing the talent show. Seeing it gives Miguel new hope.

He finally reaches Mariachi Plaza and marches straight to the gazebo where the stage manager is setting up.

"I wanna play in the plaza. Like de la Cruz! Can I still sign up?"

"You got an instrument?" the stage manager asks.

"No, but if I can borrow a guitar—"

"Musicians gotta bring their own instruments." As the stage manager starts to walk away, he tells Miguel, "You find a guitar, kid, and I'll put you on the list."

For a moment, Miguel's shoulders slump, but he will not give up. He will fight for his dream with everything he's got, so he approaches the first mariachi he sees. "Excuse me, may I borrow your guitar?"

"Sorry, muchacho."

He moves on, finding a pair of musicians practicing. "You guys have a spare guitar?" When they say no, he starts to panic. There must be someone who will lend him an instrument! He pushes his way through the gathering crowd, looking for another musician and finally finding one. "I need a guitar," he explains, "just for a little bit."

"Get outta here, kid!"

Will no one help? Miguel wonders. He hangs his head, puts his hands in the front pockets of his red hoodie, and meanders around the plaza trying to figure out what to do. If only Abuelita hadn't ruined his guitar!

Eventually, he finds himself at the statue of Ernesto de la Cruz. He looks up and gazes at the famous face. "Great-great-grandfather, what am I supposed to do?"

He half expects an answer even though the statue's made of stone, but of course, statues cannot speak. Once again, he hangs his head, but then his gaze falls upon the plaque at the base of the statue: SEIZE YOUR MOMENT. Miguel reaches into the pocket of his jeans and pulls out the photo of the headless de la Cruz with his guitar. At that moment, a firework goes off, its colorful light illuminating the skull-headed guitar that the statue holds, and Miguel gets a great idea.

He runs to the cemetery with his constant companion, Dante. When he gets there, the gravesites are decorated for Día de los Muertos with flowers and candles. Many families are gathered around. A teenaged boy reverently places a doll beside a tombstone for his sister who died very young. A family spreads a picnic blanket and enjoys pan dulce, making sure to leave some for a beloved aunt. A fútbol team gathers at a coach's grave and summarizes the latest games. A young couple shows off their toddler, bragging into the air for the ghosts of their ancestors to hear.

It's a small town. Miguel worries that someone will recognize him and tell his family where he is, so he sticks to the shadows and manages to slip by unnoticed. Finally, he reaches his destination: the mausoleum of Ernesto de la Cruz!

Miguel slinks around the side, and Dante barks excitedly.

"No, no, no, no, no! Dante, stop!" The last thing Miguel needs is attention. "¡Cállate! *Shhh!*"

He swipes a chicken leg from a neighboring grave and throws it. Dante can't resist, so he runs off. Finally, Miguel can inspect the mausoleum in peace. He peeks through the window and spots the famous guitar hanging above the crypt. More fireworks pop, and bursts of light glint off the instrument. The guitar is calling him—Miguel knows it! Instruments are meant to be played, not to be locked in a tomb, and *this* instrument, the guitar of his great-great-grandfather, is meant to be played by Miguel.

More fireworks go off, and Miguel studies the pattern by counting off the seconds between booms. Then, in perfect timing with the explosions, he throws his shoulder against the latch, breaking it so he can open the window. After glancing around to make sure no one heard, he slips into the mausoleum. The noises outside are muffled by the thick walls, and every footstep echoes eerily. He realizes he's holding his breath—because it's spooky in the mausoleum, but also because he's excited to be so close to a legend of music. After giving himself a moment to breathe, he climbs onto the crypt, slightly moving the lid and disturbing the marigold petals sprinkled about, and then comes face-to-face with the guitar. He wipes away the dust and admires the richly painted wood beneath.

"Señor de la Cruz?" Miguel says cautiously. "Please don't be mad. I'm Miguel, your great-great-grandson." He bows his head slightly. "I need to borrow this."

With his heart pounding, Miguel lifts the guitar off its mount.

"Our family thinks music is a curse," he says. "None of them understand, but I know *you* would have. You would've told me to follow my heart. To seize my moment!" He backs up a bit. "So if it's all right with you, I'm gonna play in the plaza, just like you did."

With the guitar in his hands he feels confident, as if destined for this moment. He boldly strums the guitar, but just once, because as soon as the chord sounds, the air around him vibrates, hitting him like a shock wave. The marigold petals begin to glow as brightly as the fireworks outside. Miguel shakes his head. *What just happened?* he wonders.

Then he spots light at the window. *Oh, no!* He's about to be caught! A voice from outside says, "The guitar! It's gone! Somebody stole de la Cruz's guitar! Look!"

Miguel hears keys jangling in the door. Then a grounds-keeper enters with a flashlight. "All right, who's in there?"

In a panic, Miguel sets down the guitar and puts up his hands, like someone about to be arrested. "I . . . I'm sorry! It's not what it looks like! De la Cruz is my—"

Before he can finish, the groundskeeper walks straight through him! The sensation reminds Miguel of the nausea he feels when he's on a fast carnival ride. He glances at his hands, and they are slightly transparent. *How can this be? Wait a minute.* . . . He can't believe it. He's a ghost!

The groundskeeper picks up the guitar. "There's nobody here!"

A man from outside answers, "Okay! We'll check around back."

Miguel rushes away, the whole time wondering if he's truly a ghost. It seems impossible, but it must be true, because people keep walking through him. Each time, Miguel feels sick to his stomach.

Then he hears his name. "Miguel!" When he turns, he sees Papá and Mamá, calling for him. He no longer wants to escape his family. They are the only people who can calm his fears.

He rushes to them. "Mamá!" he says, reaching for her, but it's no use. He goes straight through her, too!

"Miguel!" his father calls. "Come home! Where are you, Miguel?"

How can he live like this? Invisible, with no way of speaking to his family? This *has* to be a nightmare! He backs away, frantic, and then falls into an open grave.

"Dios mío!" a woman says. "Little boy, are you okay?" She reaches into the grave and offers a helpful hand. "Here, let me help you."

Miguel takes her hand, and she pulls him out.

"Thanks, I—"

Miguel and the woman stare at each other face-to-face, and that's when he realizes: the woman who helped him is a skeleton! He screams, and so does she. Afraid, he backs away, but then he falls backward from the shock of spotting more skeletons! As he frantically scoots away, he bumps into *another* skeleton, whose head falls off and lands in Miguel's hands.

"Do you mind?" the skeleton head says.

Miguel gasps, and the skeleton screams. "Ahhh!"

Miguel screams, too. "Ahhh!"

He throws the head, and as it tumbles away, he notices that the whole cemetery is teeming with the dead! He can't believe what he's seeing—clavicles, vertebrae, femurs, phalanges, and every single suture, fossa, and tubercle on the skeletons' bones! But perhaps the worst part is that *they* can see *him*, too! And they are just as surprised as he is.

"He can see us?"

"He's alive!"

"Impossible . . ."

"Dios mío!"

Miguel races off and hides behind a large tombstone. He frantically tries to figure things out.

"It's a dream. I'm just dreaming."

He tries to wake himself up by vigorously shaking his head. It doesn't work, so he pinches himself, and then he slaps both sides of his face. Nothing works! He's still asleep. Or maybe he *isn't* asleep. Maybe this is *real*!

Afraid but curious, Miguel peeks around the tombstone and sees the skeletons interacting with their living families. One couple dances. Another skeleton reaches for the bag of chicharrones left beside his tombstone. At his touch, the bag disappears from the land of the living and solidifies in the skeleton's hands. Miguel shakes his head again, questioning what he sees.

He stoops behind a bush and finds himself near skeletons who are gazing at the toddler he'd spotted earlier.

"Look how big she's getting," says the abuela skeleton. "She has my nose, ¿que no?"

"Don't be ridiculous," the abuelo skeleton remarks. "You don't have a nose anymore."

The abuela pokes at the big hole in the middle of her face where her nose used to be. "My lips, then. She definitely has my lips."

"If your skull-head had lips, I'd be kissing you all the

time." The abuelo stoops to kiss her, their teeth clacking as they meet.

Miguel sneaks along, hiding behind a tree to spy on a skeleton wearing a baseball cap and a whistle around his neck. He's holding a championship trophy the fútbol team left behind. *He's the coach*, Miguel realizes.

He moves on to the family having a picnic. "Here's a cuernito for Lucinda," the woman says, placing a horn-shaped piece of pan dulce before the gravesite. "They were your sister's favorite."

"No, they weren't," says the man. "She liked buñuelos." He sets down a stack of buñuelos.

"Ay!" the skeletal Lucinda says. "No one ever remembers my favorite!"

"Here, Tía Lucinda," a teenaged girl says. "A giant piece of chocolate cake."

Lucinda cheers. "Finally! My favorite dessert from my favorite niece."

The family stands to fold up the blanket, and once they've packed up, the man gets serious, and his wife and daughter put their hands on his shoulders. "I miss her. She really knew how to enjoy life."

The teenager nods. "I want to be just like her," she says, and after a solemn moment, they walk away.

Lucinda looks after them. "Well, I guess I *did* know how to enjoy life," she says. "And with these delicious desserts, I can enjoy death, too." She giggles as she takes all the snacks, and once again, Miguel is amazed when the treats disappear from the cemetery just as they materialize in her skeletal hands.

Suddenly, Dante surprises him by licking his cheek.

"Dante?!" Miguel says. "You can see me?" He feels so relieved but also confused. "W-wait, what's going on?"

Dante barks, points with his nose, and bounds through the crowd.

"Dante!" Miguel calls as he gives chase. They leap over tombstones, skid on sharp turns, and when Dante races between the legs of a man, Miguel races *through* him. *The only advantage of being invisible,* Miguel thinks, *is not bumping into people.* But then, *bam!*—he slams into a mustached skeleton with enough force to break apart and scatter all the bones.

When the head pops up, Miguel is in for another surprise. Not only does this skeleton see him, but it also knows his name!

"Miguel?!"

CHAPTER 8

"I'm sorry," Miguel says about slamming into the skeleton and scattering his bones. He frantically picks them up, and that's when he realizes that the mustached skeleton is not alone. He's with two female skeletons, and the whole group knows his name.

"Miguel?"

"Miguel?"

"Miguel?"

"You're here! *Here* here!" the mustached skull says as his bones magically pull away from Miguel's arms. One flies past Dante, who chases it, salivating. "And you can see us? Qué raro."

One of the skeleton women charges through the mustached man, scattering his bones again. "Our Migueli-ti-ti-ti-ti-to!" She grabs Miguel and squeezes him in a tight hug.

He can barely breathe, but he manages to ask, "Remind me how I know you?"

She releases him and looks him straight in the face. "We're your family, m'ijo!"

"Family?" Then Miguel recognizes her from an ofrenda photo. "Tía . . . Rosita?" he guesses.

She nods. "¡Sí!"

He turns back to the mustached skeleton, who's mostly reassembled, besides the fact that his head is turned the wrong way. The other woman straightens it. "Two inches to the left," she says. "Now two inches to the right."

"Gracias," the mustached skeleton tells her.

"Papá Julio?" Miguel guesses again. "Tía Victoria?" He recognizes all of them now. Just like in the pictures, they all wear shoemaker aprons.

Tía Victoria peers at him. "He doesn't seem entirely dead," she says, poking Miguel's cheek with a confused look on her face.

They are all so preoccupied with the bizarre family reunion, they almost don't notice when some living holiday-goers approach. They pass right through Miguel. He grabs his stomach because of how queasy he feels. "Whoa!"

"He's not quite alive either . . ." Tía Rosita adds, concerned.

At this Papá Julio starts to pace. He's clearly distressed. "We need Mamá Imelda!"

Suddenly, two identical skeletons rush over, skidding to a stop at the exact same moment. Miguel recognizes them immediately. They're his twin uncles, Tío Oscar and Tío Felipe. They're in a panic, their words rushing out.

"¡Oye!"

"It's Mamá Imelda!"

"She couldn't cross over!"

The other relatives gasp.

"She's stuck—" Tío Oscar starts.

"On the other side," Tío Felipe finishes. Then they notice Miguel. "Oh, hey, Miguel!"

The rest of the relatives turn to gaze at him. With all eyes on him, he feels like a strange new insect beneath a magnifying glass. "I have a feeling this has something to do with you," Tía Victoria says.

Tía Rosita frowns. "But if Mamá Imelda can't come to us . . ."

"Then we are going to her!" Papá Julio exclaims, his mustache flaring up. "¡Vámonos!" He grabs Miguel and pulls him along.

Miguel's a bit nervous about meeting his great-great-grandmother, because she's the one who banned music in the first place. But he can't think of anything else to do, and he can't remain a ghost, so he follows his family. They weave among the graves, carefully avoiding the living, since Miguel hates the sensation of people passing through him. Then they round a corner. . . . and Miguel is awestruck.

CHAPTER 9

"**Whoa!**" Miguel cries. A bridge, glowing with the orange petals of marigolds, arches before them. He's never seen a bridge made of petals before. It extends into the darkness, and he wonders what holds it up—there aren't any steel beams or ropes. A stream of skeletons ambles across it, the petals drifting down like orange snowflakes. Miguel's afraid that if he steps on them he'll sink through.

"Come on," Papá Julio says. "It's okay."

Miguel cautiously steps onto the bridge, the petals glowing under his feet. Amazingly, he sinks a little but does not fall. *It's like walking on pillows,* he realizes.

Then Dante rushes past him. "Dante! Dante! Dante, wait up!" Miguel calls, running after the dog and finally catching up to him at the crest of the bridge. Dante rolls in the petals and sneezes a few onto Miguel's face.

"You gotta stay with me, boy. We don't know . . ." Before finishing his thought, Miguel looks up and is awestruck once again. "We don't know where we are."

He can only gaze at something even more amazing than the bridge. Out of the mist emerges a sparkling cityscape, the Land of the Dead. It's breathtaking. Instead of sprawling outward, the city sprawls *up* with skyscrapers, centuries old. At the bottom are Aztec and Mayan pyramids. Above them are cathedrals from the colonial period, and above *them* are modern apartment buildings. All the skyscrapers are topped by cranes and scaffolds as more layers are added to accommodate the dead. The entire vista is illuminated by fireworks and strings of colorful lights outlining the buildings. Elevators, bridges, and suspended trolley cars zigzag across. This may be the Land of the Dead, but it is full of life. Miguel sees movement as skeletons and trolleys bustle about, and he hears sounds of construction, beeps and whirs of machines, and every now and then, a faint note of music.

As Miguel gazes at the fantastic view, he notices that in the arrangement of buildings and in the play of mist and light are ghostly impressions of skulls staring back at him, but they aren't threatening. Instead they seem to have welcoming smiles.

When his family catches up, Miguel says, "This isn't a dream, then. You're all really out there."

"You thought we weren't?" Tía Victoria asks.

"Well, I don't know. I thought it might've been one of those made-up things that adults tell kids . . . like . . . vitamins."

"Miguel," his aunt laughs, "vitamins are the real thing."

"Well, now I'm thinking maybe they could be."

As they move along, the twin uncles regard Miguel.

"Perhaps our young nephew can settle our debate," Tío Felipe suggests.

"Oh, yes, yes," Tío Oscar says. "For you see," he tells Miguel, "there's this new product called Velcro."

"Wasn't around when we were alive," Tío Felipe says.

"But now it's quite . . ."

". . . ubiquitous."

"So we've been wondering which makes a better fastener for shoes."

"Laces or Velcro?"

"Perhaps you can offer your expert opinion?"

"Since you undoubtedly have experience with both."

They speak back and forth very quickly, so Miguel struggles to keep up with who says what. As for their question, he's never given it much thought. Besides, how can he answer a question about Velcro when he's still trying to process the idea of talking to his dead relatives? "I'm not sure," he says.

"I can't believe how big you are," Tía Rosita interjects.

"You look like Julio when he was a boy. Doesn't he look like you, hermano?"

"He's quite handsome," Papá Julio agrees. He seems to have calmed now that they are en route to Mamá Imelda.

"We need updates," Tía Rosita decides. "Any chisme from Santa Cecilia?"

"And how is my sister, your abuelita?" Tía Victoria adds.

The twin uncles join in. "And your new primos?"

"Yes, los cuates, Benny and Manny."

Miguel tries his best to answer the questions even though he's still struggling to accept that he's talking to dead people. They seem satisfied by his answers, but then he feels a bony hand on his shoulder. It's Papá Julio. "How's your mamá Coco?" the old man asks. "I miss her very much. I can still remember how we fell in love."

Everyone anxiously waits for his answer. "She forgets things," Miguel admits. "But she hasn't forgotten any of you. I can't wait to tell her how I met everyone."

They continue along the bridge, and as skeletons pass in the other direction, Miguel receives some strange looks. A little girl skeleton points at him. "He looks funny, Mamá."

"M'ija, it's not nice to stare at—" The mother is dumbstruck when she spots Miguel. "Ay! Santa Maria!" Her eyes widen, and now *she's* the one who can't stop staring, her head turning backward to keep her eyes on Miguel as she walks in the opposite direction. Miguel feels extremely self-conscious now, so he puts up his hood to hide.

They continue toward an official-looking building on the

far side of the bridge, and that's when Miguel spots fantastical creatures. They're crawling, flying, and making nests in the architecture.

"Are those . . . ? Alebrijes!" He can't believe he's seeing living versions of the sculptures from the market. "They sell 'em in town, but those are—"

"Real alebrijes," Tío Oscar says. "Creatures of the spirit realm. Full of wonder . . ."

"Full of *something*," Tío Felipe says as an alebrije from above leaves a dropping. "Watch your step. They make caquitas everywhere."

Miguel and Dante watch a majestic horse with a lion's mane and a snake with feathers just like the famous Quetzalcoatl of the Aztecs. Like the sculptures in the market, all the alebrijes in the Land of the Dead have stripes, dots, and other designs in bright colors. Miguel could marvel at them all day.

They finally get to the end of the Marigold Bridge. As they step off, the magic of the bridge disengages. Miguel is no longer transparent and glowing. He is as solid in the Land of the Dead as he was in the Land of the Living before strumming the famous guitar.

He follows Papá Julio across the stone floor toward Marigold Grand Central Station. A voice from public speakers makes announcements: "*Welcome back to the Land of the Dead. Please have all offerings ready for reentry. We hope you enjoyed your holiday!*"

They step through a door for reentry. A row of booths

for arrivals agents separates the lobby from the city behind it. Miguel and his family search for the shortest line and take their spots. Miguel can't help standing on his tiptoes to watch the proceedings.

"Welcome back," the arrivals agent says to a traveler. "Anything to declare?"

"Some churros from my family."

"How wonderful!" the agent says. "Next! Anything to declare?"

Meanwhile, the public speakers continue the announcements. *"If you are experiencing travel issues, agents at the Department of Family Reunions are available to assist you."*

On the other side of the lobby is the departures area. Miguel watches as one skeleton after another is approved for a trip to the Land of the Living. Then he spots a skeleton being hauled away by security guards. He gives Tía Rosita a questioning look.

She shakes her head. "Oh, so sad. I don't know what I'd do if no one put up my photo."

That's when Miguel remembers why his family insists on placing photos of their loved ones on the ofrenda. The pictures are like tickets to the other side, and only those who are remembered can pass over for Día de los Muertos.

Once again, he hears: "Next!"

"Oh! Come, m'ijo," Tía Rosita says. "It's our turn."

The arrivals line moves forward. The Rivera skeletons crowd around the gate. Then the agent leans from his window. "Welcome back, amigos! Anything to declare?"

"As a matter of fact, yes," Papá Julio says, pushing Miguel to the front so the agent can get a good look at him.

"Hola," Miguel says sheepishly.

When the arrivals agent sees a flesh-and-blood boy, he shrieks and his jaw *literally* drops to the floor!

CHAPTER 10

Across the lobby, the famous Frida Kahlo waits for entry to the Land of the Living. Even though she's a beloved artist with photos in museums and private homes, she's wringing her hands and nervously tapping her foot. Her unibrow is furrowed with anxiety as she casts paranoid glances at the departures gate with its camera-mounted monitor.

"Next family, please!" the agent calls to the elderly couple at the front of the line. They stand before the monitor and it scans their faces, returning an image of their photos on an altar in the Land of the Living. "Oh," the agent says, "your photos are on your son's ofrenda. Have a great visit!"

"Gracias!" they reply.

They join the rest of their family, and as they step onto the Marigold Bridge, all of them begin to glow.

"And remember to return before sunrise," the public speakers announce. *"Enjoy your visit!"*

Frida takes a deep breath. It's almost her turn.

"Next family!" A skeleton family approaches and steps before the monitor. They have giant smiles full of braces, so it's no surprise when the agent says, "Your photos are on your dentist's ofrenda. Enjoy your visit!"

"Grashiash!" they say.

"Next!"

Frida steps up. She has brushed aside her anxiety and is full of confidence now. "Yes, it is I. Frida Kahlo." She gestures to herself. "Famous Mexican icon, beloved of the people. Shall we skip the scanner? I'm on so many ofrendas. It'll just overwhelm your blinky thingie."

"Sorry, uh . . . Miss Kahlo. Rules are rules."

The monitor scans Frida, but instead of revealing hundreds of ofrendas with her photo, an X appears, followed by a negative buzzing sound.

"Well, shoot," the agent says. "Looks like no one put up your photo, Frida."

At that, Frida rips off her unibrow and throws off her frock. As it turns out, she isn't Frida at all.

Beneath the disguise is a tall, thin skeleton. Except for the red scarf tied around his neck, his clothes are faded and threadbare. His jacket's missing a sleeve, and his pants are torn at the knees and hems. He dons a straw hat that's frayed along the brim. "Okay, when I said I was Frida . . . just now? That . . . that was a lie."

"You don't say."

"And I apologize for doing that, but it's only out of desperation. I *must* cross over."

"We go through this every year, Hector," the agent says. "Last time, you stuffed cotton in your clothes to disguise yourself as another artistic icon, Diego Rivera."

"I was trying to be gordo like him. How was I supposed to know that the stuffing would fall out?"

"Uh . . . perhaps the holes in your clothes would have provided a clue?"

Hector sighs.

"We were onto you before you reached the gate," the agent continues. "Just like the year you painted yourself as an alebrije."

"It was a genius idea, you have to admit. . . ."

"Except that you left colorful hand and footprints everywhere."

"I should have waited till the paint dried."

"And before *that*," the agent says, "you hid in a raspa cart."

Hector shivers. "Silly me. I forgot that raspa carts are full of ice. Brrr!"

"Your shivering bones were louder than the fireworks." At this, the agent laughs, but then she gets serious again. "No photo on an ofrenda, no crossing the bridge."

Hector pretends he didn't hear. "You know what," he

says, "I'm just gonna zip right over. You won't even know I'm gone."

"You know the drill," the agent says, reaching for her walkie-talkie.

Before she can call security, Hector bolts for the bridge. When he sees security guards blocking it, he splits in two, half of him going over the guards and the other half going under. Then his bones reassemble mid-flight. He's been practicing, so he doesn't miss a beat. He glances back, happy that the guards are still trying to figure out what happened.

"Almost there," Hector says to himself. He's excited. He's never made it this far. "Just a little further."

And then he arrives at the foot of the Marigold Bridge! Finally, his dream of visiting the Land of the Living is about to come true. Without hesitation, he leaps onto the marigolds— but the magic doesn't engage! Instead of sprinting across, Hector sinks right through the petals. And before he can try again, the guards saunter over.

"Upsy-daisy," one of the officers says, casually lifting Hector and pulling him back to the Land of the Dead.

"Fine, okay," Hector replies. "Who cares? Dumb flower bridge."

He shrugs it off and acts like it's no big deal, but it *is* a big deal. He *needs* to get to the other side . . . before it's too late.

CHAPTER 11

Meanwhile, a security guard escorts Miguel and his family across an arching second-floor walkway. Dante happily trots along, his tongue hanging out as he pants. "Whoa," Miguel utters as gondolas float past, each decorated with bright paint and curlicue designs. A few trolleys pass by on rickety rails, their sides plastered with movie posters and advertisements for all kinds of products, including bone polishers, splints for "unfortunate accidents," and grooming supplies for alebrijes.

Tío Felipe and Tío Oscar flank Miguel. He's still not sure who is who. In his mind, they are mirror images of the same person.

"Don't worry," one of them says. "We'll get this figured out, and then you can get back home—"

"And *we* can get back to hammering soles."

"Hammering souls?" Miguel asks nervously as he imagines his uncles beating up ghostly spirits.

"Not 'soul' as in the devil or angel on your shoulder."

"Or your sense of right and wrong."

"Your moral compass."

"Your conscience."

"And not 'sole' the fish."

"Or 'sole' the adjective, as in sole survivor, sole heir, or—"

"Sole living boy in the Land of the Dead."

"Okay, okay," Miguel says. "You mean the soles on shoes, right?"

The uncles nod, but before they can say more, they reach the doors for the Department of Family Reunions at the end of the walkway. The guard leads them into a large room with row upon row of cubicles. Frantic caseworkers punch data into computers, sift through file cabinets, answer phones, and try their best to assist disgruntled travelers.

"C'mon!" one skeleton says. "Help us out, amigo. We gotta get to a dozen ofrendas tonight."

At another cubicle, a miffed wife points her finger at her husband. "We are *not* visiting your ex-wife's family for Día de los Muertos!"

Every traveler has a problem, but no one seems as upset as the woman they're walking toward. She's in the far corner of the room, wearing a purple dress and a shoemaker's apron. She is not shy about ordering people around. "I demand to speak to the person in charge!"

A beleaguered caseworker cringes. "I'm sorry, señora. It says here no one put up your photo."

The angry traveler puts her hands on her hips as she coldly eyes the worker's old desktop computer. "My family always—*always*—puts my photo on the ofrenda! That devil box tells you nothing but lies!" In a swift movement she removes her shoe, and when she smacks the computer, Miguel can't help thinking about Abuelita slapping the mariachi. That's when he sees it. *This must be . . .*

"Mamá Imelda?" Papá Julio says.

She turns her shoe on Papá Julio, who steps back and yelps. Luckily, she recognizes him before she strikes. "¡Oh, mi familia! Tell this woman and her devil box that my photo is on the ofrenda."

Papá Julio hangs his head. "Well, we never made it to the ofrenda."

"What?!"

"We ran into, um . . . um . . ."

Mamá Imelda's eyes fall on Miguel, and as they gaze at each other, Miguel remembers her photo. She is the skeletal version of the woman who held young Coco on her lap.

"Miguel?" she gasps.

"Mamá Imelda?" He's not sure if he's supposed to hug her, shake her hand, or bow as if greeting royalty. Before he can find out, she says, "What is going on?"

Just then, a side door opens and a clerk peeks in. "You the Rivera family?"

Before they can answer, the computer short-circuits. "That's what it gets for telling lies," Mamá Imelda says with a satisfied look on her face. "C'mon," she urges, following the clerk to his corner office.

The door closes behind them, muffling the chaos of the outer room. Most of the space is in shadows, but banker lamps light the desk and reveal boxes, papers, and dusty cabinets. Through the tall windows, Miguel spots the colorful lights of the city, and occasionally a spotlight sweeps across the room.

"Well, you're cursed," says the clerk.

"What?!" Miguel exclaims. He always suspected it, but this is still terrible news.

The clerk flips through the accordion folds of a massive printout. "I pulled the record and it says here that you, uhh— Ooo-boy!—you robbed a grave?!"

The family gasps.

"We've raised a monster!" Tía Victoria cries.

"And of all nights," the clerk adds. "Día de los Muertos is a night to *give* to the dead. You *stole* from the dead."

"But I wasn't stealing the guitar!" Miguel says in self-defense.

"Guitar?" Mamá Imelda's tone suggests it's a dirty word.

"It was my great-great-grandfather's," Miguel continues. "He would have wanted me to have it."

"Ah-ah-ah!" Mamá Imelda interjects. "We do not speak

of that . . . that musician!" She cannot hide the disgust in her voice. "He is *dead* to this family!"

"Uh, you're all dead," Miguel says.

Dante stands on his back legs, and his front paws reach for the clerk's offering from the Land of the Living, a bowl of sweets on the desk.

"*Achoo!*" The clerk sneezes. "I am sorry. Whose alebrije is that?"

Miguel tries to pull Dante away. "That's just Dante."

"He sure doesn't look like an alebrije," Tía Rosita says, gesturing toward the windows, where fantastical creatures flutter outside.

"He just looks like a plain old dog," Tío Oscar says.

"Or a sausage someone dropped in a barbershop," finishes Tío Felipe.

"Whatever he is," the clerk says, "I am—*achoo!*—terribly allergic."

"But Dante doesn't have any hair," Miguel points out.

"And I don't have a nose, and yet here we are. *Achoo!*"

Mamá Imelda quickly gets them back to the subject. "But none of this explains why I couldn't cross over," she says.

Then Miguel remembers what Tía Rosita had told him earlier. In order to cross the Marigold Bridge, your picture has to be on someone's ofrenda. Mamá Imelda is right. Her family always puts out her photo, but at the moment, that photo is in Miguel's pocket. He reaches in and sheepishly pulls it out.

"Oh . . . that . . ."

"What did you do?" Mamá Imelda asks when she sees the folded picture in his hands.

Miguel wishes he could put it back in his pocket, but there's no turning back now. He unfolds it and the whole family gasps.

"You took my photo off the ofrenda?"

"It was an accident!" Miguel says.

Mamá Imelda has no time for explanations. She turns to the clerk. "How do we send him back?"

"Well, since it's a family matter . . ." The clerk flips through pages in a book of rules and proceedings. Finally, he spots the answer. "The way to undo a family curse is to get your family's blessing."

"That's it?" Miguel can't believe how easy it sounds.

"Get your family's blessing, and everything should go back to normal. But you gotta do it by sunrise."

"What happens at sunrise?" Miguel asks.

Suddenly, Papá Julio's eyes widen. "*Oh, no!* Your hand!"

Miguel looks at his hand. The tip of one of his fingers is starting to turn skeletal. How can this be? Suddenly, he knows the truth: if he doesn't return by sunrise, he'll turn into a skeleton! Miguel goes pale with shock, and he gets woozy. He's about to faint when Papá Julio catches him.

"Are you okay, m'ijo?"

Miguel nods, even though he is definitely *not* okay.

"But not to worry," the clerk says, ignoring the panicked expression on Miguel's face. "Your family's here. You can get your blessing right now." He kneels next to Tía Rosita, searching for something. "Cempasúchil, cempasúchil," he calls, as if beckoning a pet instead of a marigold. "*Aha! Perdón, señora.*" Tía Rosita titters delightedly as the clerk pulls a marigold petal from the hem of her dress.

Meanwhile, Tía Victoria crosses her arms and scoffs.

The clerk hands the petal to Mamá Imelda. "Now, you look at the living and say his name."

Mamá Imelda does as directed. "Miguel," she says, looking at him with kindness and love in spite of all the trouble he's caused.

The clerk smiles. "Nailed it. Now say: I give you my blessing."

"I give you my blessing."

The marigold petal glows in her fingers. Miguel feels hopeful. This is going to work. It must! He's about to go home. . . . But Mamá Imelda isn't finished.

"I give you my blessing to go home."

The glow of the marigold petal surges.

"To be a good boy."

It gets even brighter.

"To put my photo back on the ofrenda, and . . ." She pauses, as if making a decision. "And to never play music again."

The petal surges one last time.

"What?" Miguel pleads to the clerk. "She can't do that!"

"Well, technically she can add any conditions she wants."

Miguel stares her down, desperately wanting to challenge

the rule that she has enforced for so many years, that she *keeps* enforcing even from the Land of the Dead. But he's no match for Mamá Imelda's conviction. She's firm in her resolve.

"Fine," Miguel mutters.

The clerk nods, pleased. "Then," he says to Imelda, "you hand the petal to Miguel."

She offers it to him, and he hesitates. Can he really live without music? But if he doesn't grab the flower, he'll turn into a skeleton. He must accept her condition. He reaches, his hand trembling because he's not sure what's going to happen next. But then, the minute he grabs the petal—*whoosh!* He disappears!

CHAPTER 12

Miguel is transported to Ernesto de la Cruz's mausoleum by a whirlwind of petals. Once they settle on the ground, he checks his hands. They're back to normal! Plus, he isn't transparent anymore. He slaps his cheeks, happy to feel the stings. Then he bumps his hips against the walls. He's as solid as they are! He runs to the window and peeks out. "No skeletons!" he cheers, his voice echoing.

He laughs, relieved. He's about to run home and place Mamá Imelda's photo on the ofrenda before Día de los Muertos is over, but then . . .

He spots de la Cruz's guitar. He aches to touch it, imagining little dents in his fingers from pressing the strings.

Surely there's time for the talent show *and* the ofrenda. He knows he shouldn't disobey Mamá Imelda, but how would she know? He's in the Land of the Living, and she's in the Land of the Dead. Even if she finds out, it'll be years before Miguel sees her again, years for her to forget.

He gets a mischievous smile and grabs the guitar. "Mariachi Plaza, here I come!" he says, taking two steps toward the door before—*whoosh!*

Another whirlwind of marigolds returns him to the clerk's office, startling the family. They turn toward Miguel, his hands still in the position of holding the guitar. Miguel glances down. His hands are empty, and once again, he sees the skeletal tip of a finger. It's as if he never left.

"Two seconds and you already break your promise?" Mamá Imelda scolds.

"This isn't fair," Miguel cries. "It's my life! You already had yours!"

She takes a deep breath, and he can tell she's about to say something she's repeated many times before. "Let me tell you about my life," she begins. "When I was a young woman, I was happily married until the day—"

"I know. I know," Miguel says. "I've been hearing this story my whole life."

"That's good," she says, softening. "You should know your history. The events of the past have made us who we are today." She gestures to her family, and they nod.

"I understand why you banned music," Miguel says, "but you can't let one person ruin it for everybody. Music has good qualities, too. It makes people happy. It makes them fall in love."

"This is true," Papá Julio says. "I met Coco at los bailes—"

"*Shoes,*" Mamá Imelda interrupts, "can also make people fall in love. Just ask your abuelita and Papá Franco."

"He never got blisters," Tía Victoria says.

"And," Mamá Imelda continues, "making shoes puts food on the table and a roof over your head."

"This is also true," Papá Julio says. "We never went hungry and we always had a roof. It never leaked."

"But—" Miguel begins.

Mamá Imelda holds out her hand. "Ah-ah-ah. Let me finish. Music causes nothing but trouble. Not only did my good-for-nothing husband leave his familia, but any time someone is tempted by music, something bad happens. Our distant cousin used his money to buy a trumpet instead of a coat. Winter came, and what could he do to keep warm? He had to wrap himself in a blanket that he kept tripping over. When Papá Julio first came to our shop, he couldn't stop humming songs, and he smashed his finger in the doorway because he was too distracted by the memory of music." Papá Julio holds up a finger, and sure enough, it's a little crooked. "So you see, music brings nothing but pain to this family," Mamá Imelda says.

Miguel realizes that Mamá Imelda is as stubbornly *against* music as he is *for* it. She will never give her blessing without conditions. For a moment, he feels utterly defeated, but then he gets an idea. After all, Mamá Imelda isn't the only ancestor in the room. He grabs a marigold petal from the floor and offers it to his great-grandfather. "Papá Julio, I ask for your blessing."

The old man looks at Mamá Imelda, who hardens her brow. Cowed, he shakes his head and pulls down his hat.

"Tía Rosita?" Miguel tries. "Oscar, Felipe? Tía Victoria?"

They all refuse the petal and shake their heads.

"Don't make this hard, m'ijo," Mamá Imelda says. "You go home my way or no way."

"You really hate music that much?"

"I will not let you go down the same path he did."

Miguel turns away from the family and pulls out the photo. "The same path he did," he mutters to himself as he looks at the man with the missing face. De la Cruz's words echo in his head again: *Seize your moment. Music is in my blood.*

And it's in my blood, too, Miguel thinks. He runs his skeletal finger along the guitar in the photo. "He's family," Miguel whispers to himself.

"Listen to your mamá Imelda," Tía Victoria urges.

"She's just looking out for you," says Tío Oscar.

"Be reasonable," Tía Rosita suggests.

Miguel slowly backs toward the door. "Con permiso. I need to visit the restroom. Be right back!"

He steps out and then he hears the clerk. "Uhh, should we tell him there are no restrooms in the Land of the Dead?"

He doesn't have a chance to hear his family's answer, because he runs away. They aren't the only people he's related to. He can go to someone else, and this person will give a blessing for *everything* Miguel wants—a trip back home and music!

CHAPTER 13

By the time Coco and Julio celebrated their tenth wedding anniversary, they were skilled shoemakers. Julio took great pride in his work. He even invited his sister, Rosita, to join them in the workshop. For Coco, making shoes was a chore no different from sweeping the patio or hanging sheets on the clothesline.

Still, she enjoyed her hours in the shoemaking shop, because mixed with the factory sounds were the voices and laughter of Coco's twin uncles, her mother, her husband, her sister-in-law, and her two daughters, Victoria and Elena, who did their part by fetching water or picking up scraps that fell to the floor. Even Mamá Imelda's cat hung around, playing hide-and-seek by curling in dark corners or trotting across the overhead beams.

Coco glanced around the shop, smiling as she watched her mother going over the accounts, her uncles reviewing sketches for new designs, and Rosita teaching Victoria how to count while they inventoried the supplies. Coco was delighted to see her daughters surrounded by people who loved them. Everyone played a role in their care, even the uncles who made toys out of shoes that, for some reason or other, didn't pass Mamá Imelda's inspection. One time they put wheels on a pair of wingtips so the girls could push them around like toy cars. Another time they added long straps to ankle boots, and the girls carried them like purses. When they made slippers for the girls, they used buttons and ribbons to add faces, and instead of wearing them, the girls used them as dolls.

Coco's heart warmed when she spotted Julio with Elena. She was the youngest daughter, but she had the most passion for making shoes.

"Like this," Julio said, licking a piece of thread and guiding it through a needle.

Elena had her own needle and thread. She squinted as she aimed for the tiny hole. She kept missing, but instead of giving up, she tried harder, biting her lower lip in concentration. When she finally succeeded, Julio clapped proudly.

"Te amo, Papá," Elena said, and he kissed her forehead in response.

Now that she had children of her own, Coco understood

Mamá Imelda's strict rules. Parents often *did* know best, and they had to make decisions to protect their family, like when Coco had banned her girls from running in the workshop so they wouldn't trip over tools.

Still, when Julio taught them a new skill, Coco wondered about her own father's lessons. When Julio played with them, Coco wondered about the games she and her father had played. Even though her memory of him was hazy, she could still remember his voice and how he'd made her feel—happy and loved—the same emotions she felt when she heard music.

Coco sighed and got back to work. As she carefully carved a fleur-de-lis onto leather for some western boots, Tío Oscar peeked over her shoulder and gave an approving nod. "Don't forget to keep it damp," he said. She listened, dipping a sponge in a bucket and squeezing the excess water before moistening the leather. It was important to keep it damp, but not wet.

Once she finished carving with the swivel knife, she took the beveler tool and lightly tapped it along the design to smooth out the edges. It took a while, but eventually she finished. Then she stood up and did a few shoulder rolls to release the tension from hunching over the table so long. *One down, one to go,* she thought, because every design had to be carved twice to make a pair of shoes.

"I'm going to take a break and stretch my legs," Coco announced. "I'll bring some lemonade when I get back."

"We'll be waiting," the uncles said.

"Don't add too much sugar," Mamá Imelda advised.

Coco knew the family assumed that "stretching her legs" meant taking a long walk, but she had another idea. She snuck around the compound, pulled a tall wooden box against the wall, and used it to climb into an attic space. She had discovered the hideout years before. It was her secret, the only place where she could be herself.

She wanted to follow her mother's rules, but she couldn't ignore the rhythms that stirred in her heart, so she took off her work boots and put on the slippers she kept there. They fit snugly, and when she stood, she could feel the ridges on the floorboards.

She climbed back out of the attic and returned to the courtyard. After making sure she was alone, she tuned out the wind chimes and the distant workshop sounds, focusing instead on the memory of her father's voice as he played the guitar and sang.

Little by little, she began to dance, first swaying, then stepping side to side, and finally twirling and hopping. She made wide circles with her arms and shook her hips, the whole time imagining herself in a dance studio with her father on the stage. She began to spin—slow, slow, then speeding up, twirling faster and faster! She became a joyous blur of movement as she hopped onto the ledge of a water fountain, skipping across it and twirling again, but then— whoosh!—she lost her balance!

"Ahh!" Coco shrieked as she fell to the ground.

She felt dazed at first, and when she shook off the dirt,

she discovered that she had scraped her elbow and sprained her ankle. "Ow, ow," she said at the throbbing pain.

Soon the whole family was at her side.

"What happened?"

"We heard you scream."

"Are you okay?"

"Yes, yes," she assured them. "It was just a little tumble."

Then her mother's cat trotted up and sniffed the shoes, bringing them to Mamá Imelda's attention.

"What were you doing?" Mamá Imelda asked.

"I was just, um . . . um . . . stretching my legs."

"*How* were you stretching your legs?"

The breeze brought the sound of music from a neighboring hacienda, and Mamá Imelda scoffed. "Music!" Then a glimmer of realization crossed her face. "Were you dancing?"

Coco had no choice but to confess. "Yes, but I was dancing alone, and only after a few hours in the workshop. I wasn't neglecting my duties. Just stretching my legs, like I said. I wasn't hurting anybody."

"But you hurt yourself," Mamá Imelda said, pointing at the scrape on Coco's arm and the bruise appearing on her ankle.

Coco winced. The pain was getting intense. She'd have to ice her foot and keep it elevated for a few days.

Then she spotted her daughters. They weren't crying, but they were about to—especially Elena, with her pursed lips and furrowed brow.

"What's the matter, m'ijas?" Coco asked.

"You're hurt," Victoria said, and Elena, beside her, nodded, her face full of worry.

They let loose their tears. Coco beckoned to them, and they ran to her, falling on their knees for a group hug. She stroked their hair, trying to calm their sobs, and that's when she made a vow to herself. She would never dance again, for as much as she loved music, she loved her family even more.

CHAPTER 14

Miguel hustles down a staircase with Dante, then huddles beneath it to hide. Between the slats, he can see the upper floor where his family is already searching for him. He can tell by Tío Oscar's gestures that he's giving a description to a patrolwoman. After taking a few notes, she picks up a walkie-talkie, and Miguel nearly panics.

Breathe in, breathe out, he tells himself, hoping to calm his heartbeat. He can't hide beneath the stairs forever. Soon enough, his family will come down, and if they catch him, he'll *never* find his great-great-grandfather.

He needs an escape route, so he scopes out the area and spies an exit with a revolving door. He pulls up his hood, tightening the drawstring so that only one eye peeks out through the tiny opening.

"Vámonos," he tells Dante, and they head out. "If I wanna be a musician, I need a musician's blessing. We gotta find my great-great-grandpa."

The exit door isn't far from the staircase, the space crowded with skeletons milling about and showing off the offerings they received from the Land of the Living. Miguel carefully makes his way around them, but with everyone shifting around, it's like navigating a constantly changing maze. He has to hurry, but if he goes too fast, he'll draw attention. Twice he has close calls when he bumps into skeletons. Luckily, his hoodie provides a good disguise.

Finally, he gets close to the exit, and he's almost there when a patrolman stops him.

"Hold it, muchacho." Miguel looks up and his hoodie loosens to reveal his living face. "Ahh!" the patrolman shrieks.

Then there's a call on the walkie-talkie, and they hear a woman. "Uhh, we got a family looking for a living boy."

The patrolman wastes no time. "I got him," he says.

Miguel's pulse races again, making him wish that his chest were as hollow as the skeletons'. Surely they can hear the loud thumping of his heart! He doesn't belong here, but he can't accept a blessing with conditions. If he does, he'll never play music again. He'll be stuck making shoes for the rest of his life just like his primos, his parents, his grandparents, and all his aunts and uncles. He *must* escape.

Just then, he spots a large family approaching and takes a few sneaky steps to the side, so that when they pass, they'll create a wall between him and the patrolman.

It works, and the patrolman notices too late. "Uh, whoa. Excuse me. Excuse me, folks!" Miguel backs away as the patrolman deals with the crowd. "I'm at the Eastside exit," he says into the walkie-talkie. He keeps eye contact with Miguel, but there are still people between them. Then another large crowd arrives. Miguel continues to back away, and when he's a safe distance, he mischievously waves goodbye before sneaking into a corridor. He glances back and is relieved to discover that, for the moment at least, he's escaped.

Miguel and Dante hurry down the narrow hall, but then Dante doubles back. "Dante!" Miguel calls. He knows it's risky to retrace his steps, but he doesn't want to lose his dog, so he follows. When he catches up, Dante is at a door, sniffing the threshold. "What is it?" Miguel asks. He peeks through, but when he sees an officer inside, he hides just outside the doorway. "Shh!" he tells Dante as he tries to figure out how to escape unseen.

Meanwhile, on the other side of the door, Hector impatiently taps his foot. He's been stuck there for at least half an hour, and he can't afford to waste more time. He needs to get back to the Marigold Bridge. The Frida Kahlo costume was a fiasco, but perhaps he could try another famous person. Since he's had bad luck with artists, maybe he could be a celebrated politician or author or telenovela star. But where will he get a disguise on such short notice? He could hide in something other than a raspa cart. A golf bag? Surely his bones are as skinny as golf clubs. Or maybe he could separate himself and hide in several purses. It seems like a good idea, but what if the ladies were to go in different directions? He'd never be able to reassemble himself!

As he brainstorms, the corrections officer reviews a list of offenses. "Disturbing the peace," the officer drones on, "fleeing an officer, falsifying a unibrow—"

"That's illegal?" Hector asks.

"*Very* illegal. You need to clean up your act, amigo."

"Amigo?" Hector says, touched. He has an idea. Perhaps an emotional appeal will get him to the Marigold Bridge. "That's so nice to hear you say that, because . . ." He wipes a fake tear from his eye. "I've just had a really hard Día de los Muertos, and I could really use an amigo right now." He takes the corrections officer by the hand and is nearly overwhelmed by emotion.

The officer can barely respond. "I . . ."

"And amigos," Hector continues, "help their amigos. Listen. You get me across that bridge tonight, and I'll make it worth your while." He's not sure how he'll fulfill the promise until he spies a poster of Ernesto de la Cruz. The officer is a fan. *Perfect!* thinks Hector. "Oh, you like de la Cruz? He and I go way back! I can get you front-row seats to his Sunrise Spectacular show!"

"No, no! Oh, no no no no—"

"I'll . . . I'll get you backstage. You can meet him!" Hector says. "You just gotta let me across that bridge!"

The corrections officer pulls away, disgusted. Whatever pity he felt disappeared the moment Hector tried to bribe him. "I should lock you up for the rest of the holiday," he says. "But my shift's almost up, and I wanna visit my living family. So, I'm letting you off with a warning."

Hector stands. "Can I at least get my costume back?"

"No!"

He really wants that Frida Kahlo outfit, but he knows he should leave before the officer changes his mind. "Some amigo," he scoffs as he marches toward the door.

Miguel steps back just as the tall, lanky skeleton in tattered clothes comes out. Without hesitating, Miguel follows him down the hallway.

"Hey! Hey!" he calls out. "You really know de la Cruz?"

"Who wants to know?" the man says, turning around and shrieking when he spots Miguel. "Ah, ah! You're alive!"

"Shhh! Shhh!" Miguel says before someone hears. He glances around. So far, the coast is clear, but he can't take any chances, so he pulls the man into a phone booth.

"Yeah, I'm alive. And if I wanna get back to the Land of the Living, I need de la Cruz's blessing."

"That's weirdly specific," the man says.

"He's my great-great-grandfather."

"He's your gr-gr—whha-whaat?!" The man's jaw begins

to dislocate and drop to the floor, but Miguel catches it and pushes it into place. He can't believe how easily these skeletons fall apart, and this one seems to be falling apart physically *and* emotionally. "Wait, wait, wait, wait, wait. Wait, wait," the man gasps, turning away. "Wait, no, wait, wait, wait. Wait, wait, wait, wait, wait, wait, wait." Another gasp. "Yes! You're going back to the Land of the Living?!"

This guy's got a few screws loose, or rather, ligaments, Miguel thinks. "D'ya know what? Maybe this isn't such a g—"

The man snaps his fingers quickly, pistons firing. "No, niño, niño, niño. I can help you! You can help me. We can help each other! But most importantly, you can help *me*."

He's definitely loco en la cabeza, Miguel thinks. He peeks out from the phone booth. Bad idea! His family is coming down the staircase! Mamá Imelda spots him and heads his way.

"Miguel!" she calls.

"Ah!" he screeches.

Meanwhile, the skeleton extends his hand. "I'm Hector."

"That's nice," Miguel says, grabbing Hector by the wrist and dragging him to the exit, away from Mamá Imelda and the rest of the Riveras.

"There you are!" the patrolman calls.

Miguel speeds up, lifting Hector's hand as they run past.

"Found my uncle so we're all good now!" he explains.

He finally makes it to the revolving doors, zipping through so fast that several skeletons break apart as they slam against the glass. He feels guilty, but he doesn't have time to apologize as he rushes out. Once he exits Marigold Grand Central Station, he runs down a flight of stairs. When he's a safe distance away, he realizes that he's holding Hector's arm but missing the rest of him.

"Espérame, chamaco!" Hector calls. He catches up and says, "Now *that's* what I call a dislocated shoulder."

"Um, sorry," Miguel says, handing back the arm.

Hector reattaches it. "So why are you running away so fast?"

"Because I'm . . . I'm . . ." Miguel looks down. "I'm wanted by the authorities."

Hector shakes his head. "No need to say more. Those guys are always chasing upstanding citizens like you and me." He starts to lope off, and Miguel follows him into an alley.

"How do you get away from them?" Miguel asks.

"Most of the time, I wear a disguise." Hector glances at Miguel. "That's what you need. A disguise, so you can blend in. Right now, you got all that . . . all that . . ." He lifts Miguel's chin and turns his face left, then right. "All that *flesh.*" He thinks a moment. "You got any makeup? Face paint? Crayons? Any insects like cochineals?"

"Ugh! Why would I have bugs?"

"Just asking. They're used for making dye."

Miguel reaches into his pockets. "Will this work?" he asks, pulling out a couple of tins, one with black shoe polish and another with white.

Hector inspects it. "Perfect," he says. Then he points to a crate. Miguel takes a seat, and when Hector's bony thumb touches Miguel's face, he jumps back, afraid that being touched by a skeleton will speed up his own transformation.

"Hey, hey, hold still, hold still!" Hector quickly applies the polish. Miguel closes his eyes as the skeleton rubs polish onto his forehead and eyelids. Every now and then, Hector stands back to inspect his work. "Just a touch here," he says, "and a touch there." And finally, "Ah, ta-da!" He opens a small mirror and holds it in front of Miguel, who now looks like a skeleton. "Dead as a doorknob," Hector says, and then, "So listen, Miguel. This place runs on memories. When you're well remembered, people put up your photo and you get to cross the bridge and visit the living on Día de los Muertos." A sad shadow crosses his face. "Unless you're me."

"You don't get to cross over?" Miguel guesses.

"No one's ever put up my picture." Hector's shoulders droop, but then he brightens up. "But you can change all that!" He unfolds an old picture. In it is a young living Hector. He's smiling, dimples in both cheeks. He's got a goatee and round brown eyes that are looking dreamily toward the sky.

"This is you?" Miguel asks.

"Muy guapo, eh?"

"So," Miguel says, "you get me to my great-great-grandpa, and then I put up your photo when I get home?"

"Yes! Great idea, yes!" Hector pauses. "One hiccup: de la Cruz is a tough guy to get to, and I need to cross that bridge soon. Like *tonight*. So, you got any other family here? You know, someone a bit more . . . eh, accessible?"

"Mmmmm, nope," Miguel lies. He tries to be convincing, but he must have guilt written all over his face, because Hector is suspicious.

"Don't yank my chain, chamaco. You gotta have *some* other family."

"*Only* de la Cruz. Listen, if you can't help me, I'll find him myself." Miguel whistles. "C'mon, Dante."

He marches out of the alley, Dante padding behind. He's desperate, but he can tell that Hector is desperate, too.

"Ugh, okay, okay, kid," Hector says. "Fine . . . fine! I'll get you to your great-great-grandpa!"

Miguel can't believe it. He's finally going to meet his hero, Ernesto de la Cruz, in the flesh—or rather, he thinks with a chuckle, in the *bones*!

CHAPTER 15

"**I had him** in my sights!" Mamá Imelda exclaims. "But now he's nowhere to be found!"

The entire family had followed when she'd chased Miguel to the exit. They'd crammed themselves into the revolving door and it got stuck. Then they'd spent several minutes trying to escape. Luckily, Tío Felipe had a shoehorn in his apron and used it as a crowbar to force open the door. In their rush to get out, they slammed into each other. So now Papá Julio's and the twin uncles' bones are scattered about. They busily put themselves back together, Mamá Imelda frowning as she impatiently waits.

"Here," Tía Victoria says, adjusting Papá Julio's skull.

"I feel whole again," he says.

"And you?" Mamá Imelda asks her brothers.

They shake their heads at two patellas on the ground. "Which is mine and which is yours?" Tío Oscar asks.

"Well, I'm missing my right patella," Felipe says.

"I am, too."

"Mine's the whiter one. I polished it for the evening celebration."

"I polished mine, too."

"Hmm . . . It's a conundrum," Felipe says, "but perhaps it doesn't matter since we're identical twins."

"Of *course* it matters," argues Oscar. "You wouldn't want me to wear your chones or use your toothbrush, would you?"

Felipe squirms, disgusted at the thought of wearing someone else's underwear.

Mamá Imelda picks up the patellas. "Here," she says, handing them out. "This one's yours and this one's yours."

Felipe slaps on his kneecap. "Are you sure?"

"Of course she's sure," Oscar says. "We're as different as hammers and mallets."

"As scissors and saws?" Felipe replies.

"As wood and rubber."

"As left feet and right feet?"

"As—"

"Quiet!" Mamá Imelda says. "We have bigger worries. Where is Miguel?" She wrings her hands on her apron, distraught.

"Maybe he's at the food court," Rosita says. "I bet he's hungry, with his stomach and intestines. They're probably making all those hunger noises. Remember when we used to have stomachs that growled? Or maybe he's at the arcade trying to win a prize. The last time I was there, I won—"

"We can't stand around *guessing* where he is," Victoria interrupts. "We need a plan. We need to find him before he gets hurt."

"Ay, he is going to get himself killed," Mamá Imelda says. She paces a bit, and then she gets an idea. "We need . . . Pepita."

"P-P-Pepita?" Papá Julio stutters.

Mamá Imelda lets out a loud whistle as if calling a dog. A few minutes later, a figure sweeps across the sky, momentarily blocking the colorful lights of the city. It lands in a corner and casts its shadow on the wall. Papá Julio's bones clatter nervously when he spots the silhouette of a giant winged jaguar.

Mamá Imelda smiles. "There you are," she says sweetly. "Come to Mamá."

The creature lurches out of the shadows and into the light, baring her teeth as she roars. She's an imposing jaguar with huge wings and horns atop her head. Her long tail has scales like a dragon's, and her back feet have talons like a hawk's. Pepita's entire body is a rainbow of orange, yellow, red, green, and blue, with decorative dots and stripes. She's a real, live, giant alebrije, and though she looks frightening, she purrs contentedly when Mamá Imelda reaches up to pet her.

"We need your help, Pepita," Mamá Imelda says. "My great-great-grandson, Miguel, is lost in the Land of the Dead. Can you help us find him?"

Pepita bows in response. Mamá Imelda holds up a marigold, the same one she used to bless Miguel, and Pepita sniffs it to catch his scent.

"We last saw him here." She points to the revolving door of the exit. Pepita approaches and sniffs. She somehow catches Miguel's unique scent amid those of the hundreds of skeletons who pass through each day, and she starts meandering through the square, finally making her way to the dark alley.

"Have you found him, Pepita? Have you found our boy?"

Pepita breathes on the ground, revealing something that glows for a moment. The family leans in to inspect, everyone chiming in:

"A footprint!"

"It's a Rivera boot!"

"Size seven—"

"And a half."

"Pronated."

Mamá Imelda nods. "Miguel." She strokes Pepita's chin. "Show us more."

Pepita leans forward, and the magical glow from her breath reveals a trail of footprints. The family follows. Every now and then, Pepita stops to investigate more closely. Then she finds a wooden crate, lets out a low growl, and turns it over, revealing canisters of shoe polish.

Mamá Imelda rushes forward and picks them up. "He was here," she says. "This is definitely from the family's shoemaking shop in the Land of the Living. He can't be far. We'll find him soon, and then we can send him back to where he belongs."

CHAPTER 16

Miguel, Hector, and Dante make their way through the city, Miguel marveling at how busy it is. Santa Cecilia *never* gets this crowded, even on holidays like Día de los Muertos. Miguel's worried he'll be discovered with all these skeletons around. Like Hector said, he needs to blend in. He must look, think, and act like a skeleton, so he studies Hector's loping gait. *He walks like a monkey!* Miguel silently laughs, imitating the flappy steps and side-to-side sway.

"It's not gonna be easy, you know?" Hector says of finding de la Cruz. "You know, he's . . . he's a busy man." He glances at Miguel. "What? What are you doing?"

"I'm walking like a skeleton. Blending in." Miguel does a few goofy steps to demonstrate.

"No, skeletons don't walk like that."

"It's how *you* walk."

"No, I don't."

Miguel moves on, his arms hanging loose and his feet slapping the ground.

"Stop it!" Hector says.

Miguel laughs. He can't believe how sensitive this guy is. Then he spots a billboard advertisement: ERNESTO DE LA CRUZ'S SUNRISE SPECTACULAR! Speakers blare out his most famous song, "Remember Me."

"'Ernesto de la Cruz's Sunrise Spectacular!'" Miguel reads. "¡Qué padre!"

Hector's unimpressed. "Blech. Every year, your great-great-grandpa puts on that dumb show to mark the end of Día de los Muertos."

"And you can get us in!"

Hector gets an apologetic look on his face. "Ahhhh—"

"Hey," Miguel says. "You said you had front-row tickets!"

"That . . . that was a lie. I apologize for that."

Miguel's nostrils flare like an angry bull's. His entire future, his very *life*, depend on this plan. He gives Hector a withering look.

"Cool off, chamaco. Come on. I'll get you to him."

Miguel crosses his arms, challenging. "How?"

"'Cause I happen to know where he's rehearsing!"

Miguel doesn't trust Hector, but he's got to take a chance.

Like it or not, he doesn't know his way around the Land of the Dead, and Hector is his only link to his great-great-grandpa. So he follows him deeper into the city. They take a few escalators, hop on a trolley, climb more stairs, and eventually arrive at a warehouse. It's several stories high.

Hector snaps off his arm and uses his suspenders to slingshot it to the third floor. Once it gets there, it taps on a window, and a few seconds later, a woman opens it and leans out.

"You better have my dress, Hector!"

"Hola, Ceci!"

She lowers the fire escape ladder. Hector, Miguel, and Dante climb up. When they reach the window, Hector grabs his arm, snaps it back on, and does a few shoulder rolls. Then they climb inside, and Miguel discovers that Ceci works in a costume shop. There's a clothes rack full of dresses and a mannequin with a half-finished frock held in place by large safety pins. The cutting boards, scissors, pincushions, and fabrics remind him of the shoemaking shop back home.

"Hola," Miguel says.

"Ceci," Hector says with a shrug, "I lost the dress."

She gasps. "¡Ya lo sabía! ¡Me lo merezco por confiar en ti!"

"I know, Ceci. I know, I know, I know. Ceci . . . Ceci . . . Ceci."

"I gotta dress forty dancers by sunrise and thanks to you, I'm one Frida short of an opening number!"

Hector hangs his head and takes the scolding, while Miguel notices that Dante is wandering off. He follows, and as he leaves, he hears Hector telling Ceci, "I don't want to say this is your own fault, but you should know better than to lend me things. . . ."

Meanwhile, Dante leads Miguel to a rehearsal area with a stage. The curtains are pushed aside, revealing steel ladders to the catwalk and a row of lights. Musicians are tuning up in the orchestra pit, and someone's playing with the controls, raising and lowering a scenery lift. Workers rearrange props, and skeletons pose nude for painters.

"Dante," Miguel whispers, "we shouldn't be in here."

But Dante's too busy sniffing around. Suddenly, an alebrije monkey jumps onto his back, riding him and tormenting him with screeches and howls.

"No, no, no, Dante! ¡Ven acá!"

Dante bucks and twists like a bull, literally trying to get the monkey off his back. It works, and the monkey jumps onto the shoulder of Frida Kahlo—*the* Frida Kahlo.

Miguel finally reins Dante in, but it's too late, since Frida has spotted them.

"You!" she calls. "How did you get in here?"

"I just followed my—"

He doesn't get to finish, because Frida's eyes go wide when she sees Dante. She kneels and cups his face just like Abuelita when she's about to shower Miguel with love.

"Oh!" Frida exclaims. "The mighty Xolo dog! Guider of wandering spirits!" She pets him and laughs when he licks her arm. "And whose spirit have you guided to me?"

"I don't think he's a spirit guide," Miguel says.

"Ah-ah-ah. The alebrijes of this world can take many forms. They are just as mysterious as they are powerful."

As if to prove her point, the bright patterns on Frida's monkey swirl and he opens his mouth to exhale blue fire. Dante, meanwhile, is chewing on his own leg.

"Or maybe he's just a dog," Frida says. "Come! I need your eyes!"

Miguel freaks out. "But *I* need my eyes!"

Frida waves off his concern. "You are the audience," she says, guiding him to the rehearsal area. She holds up her hands to frame the stage. "Darkness. And from the darkness . . . a giant papaya!" Lights come up on a giant prop. "Dancers emerge from the papaya, and the dancers are . . . all me!" The dancers have unibrows and wear leotards. They crawl around the sides of the giant papaya. Behind it is an even larger half-finished mesh structure. "And they go to drink the milk of their mother, who is a cactus, but who is also me. And her milk is not milk"—Frida pauses to enhance the suspense—"but tears." She turns to Miguel. "Is it too obvious?"

He's not sure what to say. But then he never understood Frida Kahlo's art. She's got one picture of her face on a deer body—what is *that* supposed to mean? Still, she's waiting for an answer, so he has to say something. "I think it's just the right amount of obvious?" He gives it more thought. "It could use some music. Like doonk-doonk-doonk-doonk."

Frida snaps at the musicians in the orchestra pit, and they start playing a discordant pizzicato.

"Oh!" Miguel says, excited by the music. "And then it could go dittle-ittle-dittle-ittle-dittle-ittle-dittle-ittle-whaa!"

The violins follow along, Miguel smiling at the layers of sound.

"And," Frida says excitedly, "what if everything was on fire? Yes! Fire everywhere!"

The dancers gasp and freeze.

"I guess . . ." Miguel says, a bit unsure.

Frida leans in. "Inspired!" she tells Miguel. "You . . . you have the spirit of an artist!"

Miguel straightens up, proud. Yes, he's an artist. Maybe he doesn't add his face to all his pictures or replace milk with tears, but he's an artist just the same.

Frida turns back to the rehearsal. "The dancers exit," she says, "the music fades, the lights go out! And Ernesto de la Cruz rises to the stage!"

A screen emerges from a trapdoor. It's backlit, revealing the silhouette of . . .

"De la Cruz!" Miguel cheers. Finally, the moment has come. He's about to meet his great-great-grandfather! At least, that's what he thinks until a spotlight comes on. It doesn't shine on de la Cruz at all. It shines on a mannequin! "Huh?"

Frida continues to narrate. "He does a couple of songs, the sun rises, everyone cheers—"

"Excuse me," Miguel interrupts. "Where's the *real* de la Cruz?"

"Ernesto doesn't *do* rehearsals," Frida explains. "He's too busy hosting that fancy party at the top of his tower."

She gestures out a large window. In the distance is a grand estate atop a steep hill. It looks like a fancy casino with all its spotlights, statues, and fountains. At first Miguel is excited by the opulence, but then he's frustrated by how far away the estate is.

"He's all the way up there?"

Suddenly, Hector rounds the corner. He's out of breath. "Chamaco! You can't run off on me like that! C'mon, stop pestering the celebrities." He grabs Miguel's hoodie, but Miguel refuses to be pulled away.

"You said my great-great-grandpa would be here! He's halfway across town, throwing some big party."

"That bum!" Hector says. "Who doesn't show up to his own rehearsal?"

"If you're such good friends, how come he didn't invite you?"

Hector paces. "He's *your* great-great-grandpa. How come he didn't invite *you*?" He walks away from Miguel and approaches the musicians. "Hey, Gustavo!" he calls. "You know anything about this party?"

"It's the hot ticket," Gustavo answers. "But if you're not on the guest list, you're never getting in, Chorizo."

"Hey, it's Chorizo," the other musicians say, laughing. "Choricito!"

"Ha, ha. Very funny, guys. Very funny."

"Chorizo?" Miguel repeats, wondering what his favorite taquito has to do with anything.

Gustavo turns to Miguel. "Oh, this guy's famous! Go on, go on, ask him how he died!"

Miguel gives Hector a questioning look.

"I don't want to talk about it," Hector says.

"He choked on some chorizo!" Gustavo answers. Everybody laughs, including Miguel.

"I didn't choke, okay. I got food poisoning! Which is a big difference!"

Nobody seems to care. They just laugh even harder.

"This is why I don't like musicians," Hector tells Miguel. "Bunch of self-important jerks!"

"Hey," Miguel says, "*I'm* a musician."

"You are?"

"Well," Gustavo says, "if you really want to get to Ernesto, there is that music competition at the Plaza de la Cruz. Winner gets to play at his party."

"Music competition?" Miguel can't hide his excitement.

"Chamaco," Hector says, "you're loco if you think—"

"I need to get my great-great-grandfather's blessing," Miguel says, glancing at his hands. He can see even *more* bones now. If he doesn't get home before sunrise, he'll never see his living family again. He has to win that competition, and he knows he can, if only . . .

Suddenly, he remembers how Abuelita smashed his guitar right before the talent show in Santa Cecilia. And how when he went to the plaza, everyone shooed him away.

Here is another opportunity to show off his musical gift, not just for an audience but for the great Ernesto de la Cruz. Once again, he imagines himself onstage, the spotlights, the microphone, the . . .

Miguel sighs. *I really am cursed,* he thinks. *Every time I have a chance to perform, I'm stuck without an instrument.*

"You know where I can get a guitar?" he asks Hector.

Hector sighs deeply. For a moment, Miguel thinks he's out of luck, but then Hector says, "I know a guy."

CHAPTER 17

Pepita leads the Riveras through town, her magical breath revealing Miguel's footsteps. Occasionally she loses his trail because heavy foot traffic or sprinklers have erased his prints, but a few quick sniffs get her back on track. At the sky ride station, she flies across, but the rest of the Riveras have to wait for the next cable car.

For Mamá Imelda, the cars aren't fast enough. "We're wasting time!"

Eventually, Pepita leads the family to Ceci's shop, and she waits outside as they go in.

"Hola, Ceci," they say.

"Come in, come in," she says. "The shoes you made for the performance were perfect, as usual."

She's busily packing the Frida costumes so they can be delivered to the Sunrise Spectacular.

"Are these the dresses?" Rosita asks, lifting one, holding it against her, and glancing in the mirror. "It's so pretty. Can I try it on? I think I'd make a great Frida."

Victoria snatches it away. "Quit fooling around. Can't you see that Ceci's packing up?"

Mamá Imelda lifts one of the shoes and inspects it, even though she knows it's perfect, because it was made by her family. Years ago, when she had first crossed the Marigold Bridge and gazed at the maze of trolleys, the spirals of skyscrapers, and the hordes of skeletons bustling about, she'd felt lost and overwhelmed. Santa Cecilia was so small in comparison, with everybody knowing everyone. How would Imelda ever find her place in a giant metropolis like this? Then she remembered her number one rule—keep the family together. And what kept the family together? Shoes. So she set up shop, starting from scratch just like before. She still felt lonely, but making shoes gave her a purpose and a way to meet new people. Then her brothers joined her, and eventually Julio, Rosita, and Victoria. And now the Riveras had a reputation for making the best shoes in the Land of the Living *and* in the Land of the Dead.

"I gave your business cards to the dancers," Ceci says, "so you'll be getting more orders soon. They went on and on about the shoes."

"We're not here about that," Mamá Imelda says. "We're looking for a boy. A *real live* boy."

"You mean with flesh?!" Ceci asks, aghast.

"And muscles," Tío Oscar replies.

"Veins and arteries," Felipe adds.

"Stomach."

"Intestines, kidneys, lungs, and—"

"Enough!" Mamá Imelda says, and to Ceci, "Have you seen him?"

She thinks a bit. "Well, yes. A boy was here."

"With a red hoodie?" Papá Julio asks, hopeful.

"Yes, he wore a red hoodie, but . . . but . . ."

"Spit it out," Mamá Imelda says.

"He wasn't a real live boy," Ceci admits. "He was a skeleton."

"Ay, no, no, no, no, no!" cries Tía Victoria. "It's too late!"

Tía Rosita cries, too. "He's turned!" she says. "Pobrecito m'ijo!"

"We can't give up hope," Mamá Imelda says. "As long as he has a little bit of skin, a drop of blood, a single firing neuron, we can send him back." She turns to Ceci. "Which way did he go?"

Ceci points to the hallway. "I think he went to the rehearsal area. He was headed in that direction when I last saw him."

The family heads to the rehearsal area, but it's quiet when they get there. The props, instruments, dancers, and stagehands—all are on their way to the Sunrise Spectacular.

They call out Miguel's name, their voices echoing in the empty hall.

Mamá Imelda glances into the orchestra pit. "Good. No musicians," she says, "but no Miguel, either. Fan out, everybody. Search the entire area while I investigate outside."

She steps out while the rest of them search the rehearsal area. Oscar goes stage right and Felipe goes stage left. They climb metal ladders to the catwalk, peeking over, under, and around all the scaffolds.

Meanwhile, the aunts search backstage, and while Victoria looks behind curtains and beneath tables, Rosita finds a large control panel.

She pushes a button. "I wonder what this is for." Then she pulls a lever. "And how about this?" She keeps pushing buttons, pulling levers, and flipping switches. They don't do anything as far as she can tell.

"What are you up to?" Victoria says.

"I'm just playing with these buttons, trying to figure out what they do," Rosita answers, flipping another switch.

"And how is that supposed to help us find Miguel?"

Rosita shrugs.

"Stop playing around and start searching."

Rosita nods, but she can't help it. She pushes one more button, and that's when they hear Papá Julio cry out.

"Papá!" Victoria calls as she and Rosita rush to the stage.

"Down here!" he answers. "I was looking for Miguel when suddenly this trapdoor opened and I fell in."

Victoria and Rosita peek down and spot Papá Julio beneath the stage.

"Are you okay?" Victoria asks.

He nods.

"While you're down there, maybe you can search for Miguel."

Papá Julio gives her a thumbs-up, and while he's looking around, Victoria turns to Rosita.

"Let's turn on the speakers," she suggests, pointing to a switch labeled MICROPHONE and adjusting the volume knob.

"No Miguel," Papá Julio says as Rosita and Victoria push a button that lifts him through the trapdoor.

"Use the mic to call him," Rosita calls out.

Julio grabs the mic and taps it. "Testing, testing, testing." His voice echoes through the auditorium. "Miguel, m'ijo, are you out there?" No one responds. "You don't need to hide," Papá Julio says. "We're here to help you." Still nothing.

"I'm going to turn on all the lights," Victoria announces. "If he's hiding, we'll see him." She flips the switches, and every spotlight, footlight, and bulb above the rafters turns on.

"Ay!" the twin uncles cry because it went from dark to bright so quickly. "We can't see!"

Victoria and Rosita rush back to the stage. Papá Julio's shading his eyes with his hands, and all of them are squinting as they try to adjust to the sudden light. Finally, they glance up to where Oscar and Felipe hang from rungs beneath the catwalk, just like changos in a zoo. They start swinging, but since their eyes are closed, they're moving toward each other instead of moving to the sides. Before anyone can stop them, they collide, their bones breaking apart. Luckily, Papá Julio, Victoria, and Rosita step aside before getting caught in a shower of bones.

Victoria doesn't skip a beat. "Well?" she asks them. "Did you see Miguel up there? Any hints about his whereabouts?"

"No," both skull-heads say in unison.

Then one says, "It's going to take a while to figure out who's who."

"Even now," responds the other, "I can't tell whether I'm Oscar or Felipe." A couple of hands flick off the skulls' fedoras and scratch their heads as they try to work out the puzzle of their mixed-up bones.

A few minutes later, Mamá Imelda steps in and spots the twins, only half assembled. "What is going on?!" she demands, but she doesn't let them answer. "Never mind. Get yourselves together so we can find Miguel. He's not here. Pepita picked up his trail again, and you're not going to like where it goes."

CHAPTER 18

As Hector leads Miguel and Dante down a stairway, Miguel looks at his hand, turning it palm up and then palm down. It's getting bonier, and it seems to have a soft glow around it. Part of him is amazed, but most of him is frightened. Time's passing, and little by little, he's transforming from a living boy into a skeleton. He shudders as he recalls the last thing he said before leaving the hacienda: *I don't want to be in this family!* If he doesn't get back before sunrise, that's the last thing his parents will remember. It will break their hearts, and *his* heart, too.

He glances around. The stairway is steep and seems to

lead into a dark shadowy place. Soon the bright lights of de la Cruz's tower disappear behind old buildings, all in disrepair.

"How much farther?" Miguel asks.

"What, you in a hurry?"

"I'm turning into a skeleton!"

"You say that like it's a bad thing." Hector glances at Miguel, who is inspecting his bony knuckle. "We're almost to your guitar," Hector says. "Then you can perform your way to your great-great-grandpa. I'm sure it'll be lovely."

Hector jumps past the last few steps, his torso going first and the bones of his arms and legs following and reconnecting to his body one at a time.

"Keep up, chamaco. Come on!"

Miguel hops over the last steps, too, and finds himself in a shanty town. Instead of the colorful lights that brightened the upper part of the city, campfires cast flickering shadows across sooty buildings. The ground is littered with crushed soda cans, shattered tequila bottles, torn candy wrappers, and burnt-out matches. The buildings look abandoned, their broken windows revealing an even deeper darkness within. They pass a wall of graffiti—an angel falling from the sky with the words Los Olvidados—"The Forgotten."

This must be the underworld of the underworld, Miguel thinks.

Occasionally, they walk by other skeletons, but instead of gleaming white, their bones are gray and dusty—like Hector's. Still, they aren't sad. When Miguel spots a group of ratty skeletons laughing around a burning trashcan, he recognizes a camaraderie similar to that of his family as they tell jokes around the workshop.

"Cousin Hector!" the group says when they spot him, and to Dante, they say, "Hola, Pelón!" Dante trots up, yapping happily as if he's greeting old friends.

"Aay! These guys!" Hector says, nodding to a man playing a jaunty tune on a makeshift violin. Miguel guesses it's made from discarded cabinet doors, twine, and coffee cans, with a bow that looks like a pool cue snapped in two. It's roughly cobbled together, but Miguel admires it because it reminds him of his own makeshift guitar.

"Hey, Tío!" Hector says. "Your D string is sounding a little sharp."

"That's 'cause it's a piece of barbed wire!"

They laugh, Miguel joining in.

"Cousin Hector!" the ratty group cheers.

"Hey!" Hector says, waving goodbye.

"These people are all your family?" Miguel asks.

"Ahheh, eh, in a way," Hector says. "We're all the ones with no photos on ofrendas, no family to go home to. Nearly forgotten, you know?" He takes a few steps before continuing. "So, we all call each other cousin, or tío, or whatever. A pretend family's better than none at all, right?"

"I don't know," Miguel says. "Sometimes it's better not to have a family."

"You can't be serious. Why would you think such a thing?"

"Sometimes your family gets in the way," Miguel explains. "Sometimes they keep you from following your heart."

Hector stops mid-stride. Then he turns to face Miguel straight on. "Let me tell you something, chamaco. When I follow my heart, guess where it leads."

Miguel shrugs.

"It leads to my family."

"If that's true, then why are you alone?"

For a moment, Hector seems to get a shade paler, and Miguel regrets his words. He's not trying to hurt Hector's feelings. He just wants Hector to understand how he feels about his dreams. He's about to apologize, but then Hector recovers and cheers up.

"Who says I'm alone?" he says, tousling Miguel's hair. "I've got you, this little pelón dog, and all these primos in Shantytown."

He moves along, Miguel and Dante following. Eventually they find three viejitas playing cards around a wooden crate. A flashlight illuminates the game, but the battery's weak. When the bulb blinks off, the ladies shake it till it flicks back on. *Soon,* Miguel thinks, *the battery will go out completely.*

"Hector!" one of the ladies says.

"Tía Chelo! He-hey!"

He hands them a bottle of tequila. They open it and take sips, passing it along. "Muchas gracias!"

"Hey," Hector says. "Save some for me!" He examines the cards on the crate for a moment, and when the flashlight blinks out again, he shakes it for them. "Is Chicharrón around?"

"In the bungalow," Tía Chelo says. "I don't know if he's in the mood for visitors."

"Who doesn't like a visit from Cousin Hector?"

The ladies chuckle, pass around the bottle again, and hand it back to Hector. He nods a goodbye, and Miguel follows him into an alley with tarps and cardboard boxes lining the walls. About halfway down, Hector stops before a tent, holds open the flap that serves as a door, and gestures for Miguel and Dante to go inside.

Miguel shivers, because the tent looks haunted. *I'm in the Land of the Dead,* he reminds himself. *Of course it's haunted.*

He steps inside, where it's damp and quiet. As Miguel's eyes adjust to the darkness, he sees piles everywhere—stacks of mismatched dishes, a drawer full of pocket watches ticking out of sync, magazines, records, hubcaps, and deflated pelotas de fútbol. This place belongs to a collector, the stacks like miniature versions of the skyscrapers that make up the Land of the Dead. Miguel bumps into one. It teeters a bit but doesn't fall.

Hector pours the tequila into two shot glasses. Then he heads to a hammock covered with a pile of old trinkets, a dusty hat on top, and when he lifts it, a grumpy face glares back at him.

"Buenas noches, Chicharrón!" he says.

"I don't wanna see your stupid face, Hector."

"C'mon. It's Día de los Muertos! I brought you a little offering!"

"Get out of here."

"I would, Cheech, but the thing is," he gestures toward Miguel, "me and my friend here, Miguel, we really need to borrow your guitar."

"My guitar?"

"I promise we'll bring it right back."

Chicharrón bolts up, the pile of trinkets falling off the hammock. "Like the time you promised to bring back my van?" he asks, incensed.

"Uh . . ." Hector says.

"Or my mini-fridge?"

"Ah, you see . . . uhhh . . ."

"Or my good napkins? My lasso? My femur?!"

"No," Hector says, "not like those times."

For a moment, Miguel thinks Chicharrón is going to swat Hector with his femur. Instead he raises a finger to give a tongue lashing, but before he can say another word, he slumps weakly and collapses back into the hammock, a golden flicker flashing through his bones.

Hector rushes forward. "Whoa, whoa! You okay, amigo?"

"I'm fading," Chicharrón says. "I can feel it." He glances at his guitar. "I couldn't even play that thing if I wanted to."

Hector's eyes dart from Chicharrón to the guitar. "Well, since you're not using it." He reaches for the instrument.

"Hector," Miguel says, "maybe you shouldn't." He really

wants the guitar, but not like this. He can tell that Chicharrón's sick, that the guitar gives him comfort.

"Shh, shh, shh, shh," Hector whispers. Then he tunes the guitar, and to Chicharrón, he says, "Any requests, my friend?"

"You know my favorite, Hector."

Hector plays a few opening notes and starts a lovely, lilting tune. Chicharrón nods to the beat and smiles. Meanwhile, Hector begins to sing a silly song about a girl named Juanita. Miguel stares at him in amazement. *Hector is a musician?*

When Hector gets to a funny part of the song, he pauses to glance at Miguel, his hands still strumming. He adjusts the lyrics.

"Those aren't the words!" Chicharrón says.

"There are children present," Hector explains before continuing with the final verse.

He holds on to the last syllable and then finishes with a soft flourish on the guitar. Miguel is surprised. This guy has talent!

He can tell Chicharrón thinks so, too. The old man is tickled and joyful with no sign of the grumpy face that had greeted them a few minutes before. For a moment, he seems healed and fully alive. "Gracias," he says. Then he closes his eyes, at peace.

Suddenly, the edges of Chicharrón's bones begin to glow with a soft, beautiful light. Then . . . he dissolves into dust.

Miguel shakes his head and rubs his eyes, as if to double-check what he just saw. But Hector doesn't seem surprised.

He looks at the empty space—first with sadness and then with respect. He picks up a shot glass, lifts it in Chicharrón's honor, and drinks. Then he places it, rim down, next to Chicharrón's glass, which is still full.

"Wait," Miguel says, "what happened?"

"He's been forgotten," Hector sighs. "When there's no one left in the living world who remembers you, you disappear from this world. We call it the Final Death."

"Where did he go?" Miguel asks.

Hector shakes his head. "No one knows."

Miguel considers this. When he first arrived in the Land of the Dead, he was pleased to learn that his departed ancestors were still out there, enjoying themselves and having new adventures. He can't believe they'll completely disappear someday. That's why the pictures on the ofrenda are so important, he realizes. All these years, he put them up without questioning why, a mindless habit. Now, for the first time, he's truly grasping the significance of his family's traditions.

All these piles in Chicharrón's tent, they were a desperate attempt to hold on to life, but no amount of stuff can equal a loved one's memory.

"But *I've* met him," Miguel says about Chicharrón. "I could remember him, when I go back."

"No, it doesn't work like that, chamaco."

"Why not?"

"Our memories," Hector explains, "they can only be passed down by those who knew us in life. In the stories they tell about us. But there's no one left alive to pass down Cheech's stories." His voice is full of remorse, and Miguel realizes why he's so desperate to cross the Marigold Bridge.

"You're about to be forgotten, too, just like Chicharrón."

Hector nods and sighs heavily, but then he puts a reassuring hand on Miguel's. "Hey," he says, his old cheerful self again, "it happens to everyone eventually." He gives Miguel the guitar. "C'mon, de la Cruzcito. You've got a contest to win."

Hector throws aside the curtain and exits. Before heading out, Miguel glances at the shot glasses—one empty, the other full. Now he's got *two* reasons to return home—to save himself from turning into a skeleton, and to save his friend from turning into dust.

CHAPTER 19

On the other side of Shantytown, the Riveras tiptoe down the dark stairway. When they reach the bottom, they take a minute to observe their surroundings.

"You're right," Papá Julio says to Mamá Imelda. "I don't like where this trail has taken us."

"It's so gray," Tío Felipe says.

"And dusty," adds Oscar.

Tía Victoria runs her finger along a wall. It's black with soot when she turns it over.

"I was hoping to avoid this place for many years to come," Mamá Imelda says.

Papá Julio turns back to the stairs. "Good idea. Why don't

we avoid it right now? It's . . . it's . . . it's haunted! And you know me, I'm scared of ghosts."

"You *are* a ghost," Tía Rosita says.

"Well, then," he replies, "I guess that makes me scared of myself."

Pepita roars to get their attention. Her colors are even more brilliant against the gloomy background.

"What is it?" Mamá Imelda asks. "Have you found Miguel's trail?"

Pepita exhales, but when the cloud of breath floats away, it reveals nothing. She lifts her nose to the sky and sniffs around, but she fails to catch Miguel's scent.

"Maybe he isn't here?" Papá Julio says, one foot on the stairs.

"No, no, no," Mamá Imelda says. "He's near. I can feel it in my bones."

"Then why can't Pepita find his footsteps or catch his scent?"

"Because," she explains, "this is the land of the forgotten. Nothing here lasts for very long."

"Including us," Papá Julio says. "That's why we should leave right now."

She ignores him. "We'll have to do this the old-fashioned way, by using our own tracking skills." She looks to the right, then left. She hushes everyone and closes her eyes to listen. "I hear"—she turns her head slightly—"music. And if I know Miguel, that's where he went."

She leads the way, the other Riveras and Pepita following.

As the music gets louder, Tía Victoria and Tía Rosita absentmindedly hum along, their feet stepping to the beat. Then Mamá Imelda turns sharply, hands on her hips. "You know the rules."

"Yes, but we can't help it," Rosita says, "because . . . well . . . it's like this. I like making shoes, but I might like it *more* if I could sing while working."

"Me too," Victoria adds, for once agreeing with her aunt.

"Me three," the uncles say in unison.

Mamá Imelda dismisses them. "That's ridiculous. Everyone knows that singing while you work hampers productivity." She stares at them until they all nod in agreement.

The group continues on its way, eventually reaching the ragtag musicians huddled around the burning trashcan. When they see the family, they stop singing, mid-note, and the lead musician says, "Buenas noches."

"Hola," the Riveras say in unison.

He tips his hat. "And how may we help you? You are amazingly"—he hunts for a word—"*solid* for this part of town." He and his friends glance at their own bones for contrast. Not only are they dusty and brittle, but they are also slightly transparent.

Mamá Imelda says, "We're looking for—"

"You look familiar," the musician interrupts. "I've seen your picture. Where did I see it?" He snaps his fingers a few times as he tries to remember.

Mamá Imelda shrugs it off. "You probably saw my picture on an advertisement. My whole family is famous for making shoes. Riveras make the best shoes in both the Land of the Living *and* the Land of the Dead."

"Famous shoemakers, eh? Perhaps you can help us out. We haven't had a good pair in many years." The ragtag musicians lift their feet. Sure enough, the soles of their shoes hang open.

The uncles lean over to examine. "Too threadbare to fix, but perhaps we can offer some duct tape?" Oscar reaches into a pocket and pulls out a roll.

The leader takes it. "Pos, it will have to do." He starts wrapping duct tape around his shoe and repeats his earlier question. "And how may we help such fine, solid-looking people like yourselves?"

"We're searching for a boy," Mamá Imelda says. "Have you seen him?"

"He's with a little Xolo dog," Rosita adds.

"Sí, sí, with Pelón." He hands the duct tape to another musician, and he points. "They went that way."

"Gracias, gracias," the family says as they head off in that direction.

A few minutes later, they hear the musicians singing again, but soon the voices fade away. Then they pass a crate with a dead flashlight and a haphazard arrangement of cards. They also pass a campfire in the middle of the street. It has a grill with a can of beans bubbling over. When a letter flies by, Victoria catches it. *"Dear . . ."* it says, and nothing more. They turn into an alley and observe a rocking chair with a half-finished mitten on the seat.

"Ay, los pobrecitos," Tía Rosita says. "They turned to dust right in the middle of knitting or playing cards or heating beans."

"I wonder what this letter was going to say," Victoria adds, turning it over.

"We'll never know," Rosita says. "It's like an unfinished story."

Oscar says, "I would hate to experience the Final Death—"

"Right in the middle of making shoes," Felipe finishes.

"I want my Final Death to be just like my first one," Papá Julio says. "With Coco by my side."

There's a moment of silence as they remember Coco. Then Mamá Imelda whispers, "Listen." She turns her head this way and that. "I hear flapping." She follows the sound, eventually arriving at Chicharrón's tent, the loose curtain swaying in the wind.

The family enters, sidestepping around the piles.

"Look at all these wonderful items," Rosita says.

"You mean, junk," Victoria says.

"Oh, no," Rosita says. She points to a stack of newspaper. "I could use those for giftwrap, and those"—she points to a pile of hubcaps—"can be for giant wind chimes. And—"

"Like I said, it's all junk," Victoria repeats. "And instead of thinking about things to make, we should be searching for Miguel."

The family inspects the entire tent, even the spaces behind the flaps. Mamá Imelda notices that mixed with the random items are a bowl of guitar picks, a box of sheet music, amplifiers, snapped nylon strings, and a broken metronome.

"Everything but the guitar," she observes. "Somehow Miguel found this . . . this . . . *musician*"—she nearly spits the word—"and took the guitar for himself. It's the only thing that makes sense."

At that moment, Pepita peeks in and beckons them outside. They follow her, and halfway up the alley, the magical jaguar breathes, revealing, once again, Miguel's footprints.

"This is excellent news," Mamá Imelda says. "His prints have not yet disappeared, which means he was here a short time ago."

Pepita continues to breathe, revealing a path that leads them to . . .

CHAPTER 20

"**A trolley!**" Miguel shouts gleefully. He's having a great time climbing over seats, running through the aisle, and finally hanging off the back, where Hector idly fiddles with the guitar. Dante sticks his head out a window, his tongue flapping and eyes squinting in the wind. Miguel laughs. Why do dogs love to stick their heads out of moving vehicles?

"The A string is still off," Hector mutters to himself as he turns the tuning peg.

"You told me you hated musicians," Miguel says. "You never said you *were* one."

"How do you think I knew your great-great-grandpa? We used to play music together. Taught him everything he knows." Hector shows off with a fancy riff but botches the last note.

"¡No manches! You played with Ernesto de la Cruz, the greatest musician of all time?"

"Ha-ha! You're funny! Greatest *eyebrows* of all time maybe, but his music, eh, not so much."

How could he say that? De la Cruz is a great musician! "You don't know what you're talking about," Miguel says.

"Okay, Mr. Expert. What's so great about it? I'm all ears. Well, that's figurative, because I don't have any—"

"Yeah, I got it," Miguel says, anxious to defend de la Cruz. "I listen to his music and . . . it's like, he gets me, you know? Even though I've never met him."

"Well, I *have* met him," Hector says, "and honestly, I don't think he'd care for you." When Miguel gets a hurt look on his face, Hector playfully punches him. "I'm kidding!"

Miguel tries to laugh it off, but he can't. "What if you're right?" he says. "What if I finally meet my great-great-grandfather, and he doesn't like me?"

"Ay, chamaco, what's not to like? You're a cool kid."

"I am?"

"Well, technically speaking, you're a *warm* kid, on account of having blood and veins and . . . and . . . *flesh.* But you know what I mean. You're interesting, fun, and talented. He's going to *love* you. Trust me."

"You think he'll let me play music? You think he'll teach me?"

"Of course. That's what great-great-grandpas do."

Just then, the trolley abruptly stops, making them stumble a little. As they step off, Hector gestures to the area at which they've arrived. "Welcome to the Plaza de la Cruz!" he says. "Showtime, chamaco!"

The plaza lives up to its name. There's a giant statue of de la Cruz in the center. Kiosks along the periphery sell refrigerator magnets, shot glasses, tote bags, postcards—all featuring de la Cruz. Even the tambourines bear his face. "Llévalo!" a vendor calls. "T-shirts! Bobbleheads!" Children play with de la Cruz marionettes, the wooden hands strumming guitars. A pyrotechnic bullfight ignites the air. Skeletons dance, sip aguas frescas, and wave sparklers and glow sticks in fluorescent pinks and greens. Nearly every instrument is there—guitars, drums, violins, and trumpets—bandolóns and bajo sextos—harps, lutes, and didgeridoos. One lady scrapes out rhythms on an old washboard while a man uses trash can lids for cymbals. Miguel is amazed to learn that almost anything can be made into an instrument. For a moment, he forgets his family's ban on music as he imagines making instruments from items in the shoemaking shop.

He and Hector make their way to an elevated stage, a crisscross of beams beneath it. On top of the stage are a microphone, a drum set, a row of multicolored floor lights, and giant speakers. A banner proclaims BATTLE OF THE BANDS!

Then the emcee steps up to the mic. Her green hair is combed into a tall updo with flowers and tiny calaveras tucked between the strands. She's wearing an off-the-shoulder gown with a high slit to show off the gleaming white bones of her legs. She's got a necklace of flowers, and petals painted around her eye sockets. She's the most glamorous skeleton Miguel has ever seen.

"Bienvenidos a todos!" she says. "Who's ready for some música?" The audience whoops and cheers. Miguel joins in, loving the excitement. "It's a battle of the bands, folks. The winner gets to play for the maestro himself, Ernesto de la Cruz, at his fiesta tonight!" More whooping. More cheering.

"That's our ticket, muchacho," Hector says, and Miguel responds with a determined nod.

"Let the competition begin!" the emcee announces.

The first act is a tuba and violin duo. Miguel wants to watch, but Hector pulls him away, telling him they need to sign up to compete. They head backstage, and as they wait in line, Miguel taps his foot and hums along as various acts perform. There's a saxophone player, a hard-core metal band, a choir, and plenty of mariachis. There's a guy who plays marimba on the back of a giant iguana alebrije, a DJ with an electronic keyboard, and a group of nuns playing accordions. When a dog orchestra performs, Miguel wonders if Dante has any musical talent.

Finally, he and Hector sign in. The contest director slaps numbers on their backs, and Miguel realizes it's time to stop acting like a member of the audience and start acting like the performer he wants to be.

"So what's the plan?" Hector says. "What are you gonna play?"

"Definitely 'Remember Me.'" Miguel plucks out the beginnings of the song's guitar solo. He knows it by heart. He's about to sing the first verse when Hector clamps his hand over the fretboard.

"No, not that one. No."

"C'mon," Miguel says. "It's his most popular song!"

"Ehck, it's too popular. That song has been butchered enough for a lifetime."

Miguel's about to protest, but then he realizes that several groups are rehearsing. He hears a tone-deaf voice drone the familiar lyrics, and an opera singer's soprano pierces through the crowd with another rendition of the song. One guy plays water glasses to the tune, and another blows it out on a kazoo. Hector's got a point, so Miguel says, "Well . . . what about . . . 'Poco Loco'?"

"Epa! Now you're talking!"

Then a stagehand calls out, "De la Cruzcito?"

"Sí?" Miguel responds.

"You're on standby!" the stagehand says, and to another band, "Los Chachalacos, you're up next!"

An impressive band steps onto the stage. They have everything—strings, percussion, horns. They must be a crowd favorite, because everyone starts cheering, "Chachalacos!" The band bursts into a mighty intro and the audience goes wild. They're so polished, playing with all their heart and bone marrow. When Miguel peeks out and sees the frenzied audience waving their glow sticks in the air, he feels sick to his stomach and starts to pace, all fidgety.

The more he processes the situation, the more nervous he gets. What was he thinking? Just because he can play alone in his hideout doesn't mean he can play in front of an audience. He sounds good to himself, but does he sound good to other people? Except for Dante and Mamá Coco, who loves him no matter what, no one's heard him sing. Will he make a fool of himself if he goes out there?

"You always this nervous before a performance?" Hector asks.

"I don't know. I've never performed before."

"What?! You said you were a musician!"

"I am!" Miguel says, but then he checks himself. "I mean, I will be. Once I win."

"That's your plan?" Hector's voice cracks with exasperation. "No, no, no, no, no. You have to win, Miguel. Your life *literally* depends on you winning! And you've never done this before?" He takes off his hat, then puts it back on, then takes it off again. Hector reaches for the guitar. "Gimme the guitar. I'll go up there."

Miguel recoils, refusing to hand over his instrument. "No."

"This isn't playtime, kid."

"I need to do this," Miguel says.

"Why?"

"If I can't go out there and play one song, how can I call myself a musician?"

"What does that matter?" Hector says, his voice more frantic as he glances at the stage.

"'Cause I don't just want to *get* de la Cruz's blessing. I need to prove that"—he hesitates—"that I'm *worthy* of it."

"That's such a sweet sentiment," Hector says, "at *such* a bad time."

He studies Miguel, and the boy straightens up, firm in his decision to perform.

"Okay, okay," Hector says, softening. "You wanna perform? Then you gotta *perform!*"

Miguel smiles, excited and surprised that Hector wants to help.

"First you have to loosen up," Hector says. "Shake off those nerves!" He does a loose-bone skeletal shimmy, and Miguel copies the move. "Now give me your best grito!"

"My best grito?"

"Come on, yell! Belt it out! Ooooooh he-he-hey! Ah, feels good! Okay, now, now . . . now you."

"A . . . A . . . Ayyyyy yaaaaayyyay . . ." Miguel tries, sounding like a squeaky rocking chair.

Dante whimpers. *Great,* Miguel thinks, *even my dog is unimpressed.*

"Oh, c'mon, kid," Hector says, but Miguel can only shrug. "Okay, okay. Here's another bit of advice. Works for me every time."

"Another idea?" Miguel asks, hopeful.

"Oh, yeah. The secret to all the great operas, ballads, hymns, lullabies—" He's interrupted when Los Chachalacos wraps up to raucous applause. "The secret to all the great performers throughout the world, throughout history, beyond—"

"What is it?" Miguel demands, because the audience is starting to quiet down.

"Love," Hector says. "When you go out there, ignore all those strangers in the audience and pretend like you're singing to someone you love." He gets a dreamy look in his eye.

"Who do *you* remember?" Miguel asks.

Hector sighs. "She's still in the Land of the Living. Every time I sing, I pour all my love into each note, hoping my voice will cross the Marigold Bridge and reach her, if only in her dreams."

Before he can say more, the stagehand calls, "De la Cruzcito, you're on now!"

Miguel's eyes go wide, and he gulps.

Hector takes his shoulders. "Miguel, look at me."

"Come on, let's go!" the stagehand says.

"Hey! Hey, look at me." He looks directly into Miguel's eyes. "You can do this. Sing to someone you love, grab their attention, and don't let it go!"

Miguel hears the emcee's voice announcing, "We got one more act tonight, folks."

"Hector?" he says, still seeking advice.

"Make 'em listen, chamaco! You got this!"

"¡Damas y caballeros!" the emcee says. "De la Cruzcito!"

The crowd applauds, and before Miguel can take another breath, he's led onto the stage.

CHAPTER 21

Coco sat before the mirror in her room and wondered, *Where did the years go?* She was an old woman now, the oldest person in the Rivera family. Her eyes couldn't see well anymore, her hands were getting arthritic, and her whole body ached when stooped over a workbench for too long, so Coco had stopped making shoes. Besides, she had great-grandchildren now, and it made more sense to babysit while their parents worked in the shop.

Someone tapped on her bedroom door. Then she heard Elena stepping in. "Hola, Mamá. Ready?"

Coco nodded. Because of her stiff hands, she struggled to make her braids, so each morning, Elena made them for her. As her daughter brushed out the tangles and talked about current shoemaking projects, Coco remembered her days in the shop and wondered how many shoes she'd made in her lifetime. It was impossible to know. She could only remember the first pair, the last pair, and the special ones in between. For Elena's wedding, Coco had taken tiny sequins and beads, carefully gluing them to the satin pumps to create an intricate floral design. She'd also made patent leather dress shoes for Julio. He wore them on special occasions, and when he died, Coco tenderly polished them for his funeral. Even now, it made her smile to know he was buried in shoes made with love.

"Ouch!" she cried when Elena pulled at a tangle snagged in the comb.

"I'm sorry," Elena said. "I didn't mean to pull your hair."

"It's okay. I know it was an accident."

Elena returned to her task, this time parting the hair straight down the middle and separating it for braids. When Coco closed her eyes, Elena said, "Why do you close your eyes when I start making the braids?"

Coco laughed, a little embarrassed. "I pretend I'm a child again and that Mamá Imelda is fixing my hair." She opened her eyes and caught Elena's gaze in the mirror. "You have her touch."

Elena beamed. "I do?"

"Yes, m'ija. You remind me so much of your mamá Imelda."

Elena paused a moment. Then, as she got back to work,

she said, "Isn't it strange how I'm brushing your hair just like Mamá Imelda did when you were a child? And how someday, my daughter will probably brush *my* hair?"

Coco nodded. "The circle of life," she said.

Just then the door flew open, and Abel and Rosa rushed in. Rosa immediately crawled under the bed and chanted, "Find me. Find me," because hide-and-seek was her favorite game. Meanwhile, Abel bounced off the wall—*literally*. He loved to slam against walls, punch pillows, and kick rocks on the ground. He wasn't angry or violent, just full of boisterous energy. Thank goodness he spent his days in school, because Coco could not keep up with him.

"Mucho cuidado!" Elena warned as he was about to crash into a wall again.

"There you are," Berto said as he stepped in and marched right up to Abel. "How many times do we have to tell you? No running indoors." At that, Abel ran out of the room. "Where are you going?" Berto called after him.

"I can't run inside, so I'm going to run outside instead!"

Before Berto could chase him, Rosa said, "Find me. Find me."

Berto put his hand on his chin. "Hmmm . . ." he said. "Where is my daughter? My beautiful Rosita? Did she run in here?"

He winked at Mamá Coco, and she played along. "Oh, no. I haven't seen her all day."

"I don't think she's here," added Elena.

They heard giggling from beneath the bed.

"Well, maybe I should have a look, just in case." Berto pulled back the covers, peeked behind the bedframe, looked in the closet, and peered under every piece of furniture except the bed. "I wonder where she could be."

That was Rosa's cue. She crawled out and victoriously announced, "I won!"

Berto tickled her, gave her a kiss, and told her to stay with Mamá Coco while he walked Abel to school. Then he left, nearly bumping into Luisa, who was stepping in, an infant cradled in her arms.

"Abel's late for school," Elena said to explain why he was rushing away so fast. She had just finished the second braid and was securing the end with a rubber band.

Then she and Coco went to Luisa to fuss over the infant. He was awake and his eyes flitted from person to person. Mamá Coco held out a finger, and he clasped it with his tiny hand. How Coco loved the strong grip of her new great-grandson, Miguel.

After a few more minutes, Elena said, "Well, it's time to get to work."

Luisa gave the baby to Mamá Coco. "I'll be back in a couple of hours to feed him."

Mamá Coco nodded as she took Miguel in her arms.

After the ladies left, Rosa ran to the corner where they kept a box of toys. She toppled it over and grabbed wooden blocks and action figures from her favorite cartoons. As she busily made a tower with the blocks, Coco settled in her rocking chair.

She began rocking Miguel, the chair's soft creaks like the gentle beat of a lullaby. It wasn't a dance, but the rocking chair felt just as musical. Coco glanced at her door, toward the shoemaking shop. *They can scold me all they want,* she thought, *but no one's going to keep me from humming to the little ones.* So she hummed. Rosa was too preoccupied to notice, but Miguel seemed energized by the tune.

"You like the song?" Coco asked.

He couldn't talk yet, but he tried to utter his first sounds—"goo, goo." Then he moved his little arms, and even though Coco knew the moves were random, she couldn't help comparing him to the conductor of an orchestra.

"Heh, heh," she laughed. "You have music in your blood, don't you?" She gently stroked his cheek. "You are just like my papá."

As she continued to rock and hum, she remembered her conversation with Elena, and she smiled at the thought of her mother and father returning in the habits and talents of their descendants.

Miguel went "goo-goo" again, and this time she knew. This tiny boy wasn't trying to talk—he was trying to sing.

CHAPTER 22

Miguel stumbles onto the stage, guitar in hand. He squints beneath the blinding lights. He's as quiet and motionless as the statue of de la Cruz. He's pale and trembling, as if he's seen a ghost. But of course! He *has* seen a ghost! He's seen hundreds of ghosts today.

The crowd begins to murmur impatiently. "Bring back the singing dogs!"

Miguel looks to Hector in the wings. His friend does the "loosen up" bone shimmy, so Miguel does it, too. Next Hector takes a breath deep into his chest, gesturing for Miguel to do the same. Miguel turns back to the audience, closes his eyes, takes a deep breath, and . . .

"Haaaaaai-yaaaaaaaaaaai-yaaaaaaaaai!" Never before has he belted out such a loud, full-throated, resonant grito!

Members in the audience return the cry, while others applaud. The noise shocks Miguel out of his paralysis, and suddenly he remembers where he is and what he's supposed to do—win this contest so he can meet his great-great-grandfather and get his blessing. Remembering Hector's advice, he thinks about someone he loves—Mamá Coco—and he strums the opening notes, then begins to sing "Poco Loco." He imagines the lyrics as he says them, describing how love can make the world topsy-turvy, how it can make people just a little bit crazy.

The audience perks up. People sway to the beat, tap their feet, and snap. They're smiling! No wonder Ernesto de la Cruz loves to perform in front of live audiences. It brings so much joy!

During the musical interlude, Dante drags Hector to the stage, and Miguel finds himself with a partner beneath the spotlight. His friend warms up and then busts out some percussive footwork to accompany the guitar.

"Not bad for a dead guy!" Miguel tells him.

"You're not so bad yourself, gordito! ¡Eso!"

Hector gets creative with his dancing. He takes off his head and shakes it like a maraca. He twirls his bony limbs and uses two ribs as drumsticks. The audience hoots with glee!

Miguel glances at him, and Hector winks back. Music is best when shared, and here they are sharing it with a live audience and with each other. Finally, Miguel can play openly and with someone who understands that music isn't just about notes and chords—it's about heart!

Hector sings one line; Miguel sings another. Then they croon in unison. Miguel can feel their voices fit together, like pieces in a puzzle.

The audience claps, keeping time with the song, and Dante lets out a harmonious howl.

Meanwhile, near the entrance, a ripple of glowing footprints leads Pepita and the Riveras to the plaza. That's where they lose track again. Too many people are masking the trail.

"He's close," Mamá Imelda says. "Find him." She and Papá Julio scan the edge of the audience, while the rest of the Riveras squirm their way into the crowd. Tíos Oscar and Felipe flank groups of people and say, "We're looking for a living kid . . . about twelve?" Tía Victoria tugs at shirts— "He's about this tall and wearing a hoodie?" Tía Rosita taps shoulders—"Have you seen a living boy?"

They aren't having any luck. Everyone just shrugs or shakes their heads.

"C'mon," Mamá Imelda says to Papá Julio. "Let's find someone in charge."

Back onstage, Miguel and Hector sing the final words. They hold the last syllable of the song, raising the volume for a grand finale. Then they wrap it up with one more heartfelt grito and the audience erupts into applause.

Miguel smiles, soaking in the moment. He did it. He got over his stage fright and performed. For a few minutes, he completely forgets about his problems. The only thing that matters is the music and making others happy. Finally, he feels like a true musician. And it feels like something he was born to do!

Hector slaps him on the back affectionately. "You did good! I'm proud of you!"

Miguel swells at his accomplishment, and he takes a bow, the audience going wild. But then he spots Tío Oscar and Tío Felipe talking to strangers. He looks a few feet over, and there's Tía Rosita talking to someone else. He glances stage right and sees that Papá Julio's with the emcee!

"Otra! Otra! Otra!" the audience calls.

Miguel doesn't have time for an encore. In a panic, he pulls Hector off stage left, away from Papá Julio. He quickly finds a hiding spot behind some electrical equipment.

"Hey, where are you going?" Hector asks as he tries to pull back.

"We gotta get outta here."

"What, are you crazy? We're about to win this thing!"

There's an ear-piercing screech from the microphone. Then the emcee comes on. "Damas y caballeros, I have an emergency announcement. Please be on the lookout for a living boy, answers to the name of Miguel. Earlier tonight, he ran away from his family. They just want to send him back to the Land of the Living." A rumble of concern rolls through the audience. The emcee continues, "If anyone has information, please contact the authorities."

Hector's eyes go wide. Miguel can tell he's figured out the situation. "Wait, wait, wait!" Hector says. "You said de la Cruz was your *only* family. The *only* person who could send you home."

"I do have other family, but—"

"You could have taken my photo back this whole time!"

"But they hate music," Miguel tries to explain. "I need a *musician's* blessing!"

"You lied to me!"

Miguel gets defensive. "Oh, you're the one to talk!"

"Look at me," Hector says, holding out his arms. "I'm being forgotten, Miguel. I don't even know if I'm gonna last the night!" He gets a determined look on his face. "I'm not gonna miss my one chance to cross that bridge 'cause you want to live out some stupid musical fantasy!"

"It's not stupid!" Miguel says. When he discovered Hector's talent, he thought his new friend would understand. How can a man who knows how to sing, dance, and cure stage fright think that music is stupid?

Hector grabs Miguel's arm and pulls him toward the stage. "I'm taking you to your family."

"Let go of me!"

"You'll thank me later."

Miguel yanks his arm free. "You don't wanna help me. You only care about yourself! Keep your dumb photo!"

He pulls the photo from his pocket, glancing one more time at the happy face of a living Hector. *He's just like my family,* Miguel realizes. *He thinks he knows what's best for me, without asking what I want.* Feeling betrayed, he throws away the picture. A breeze catches and carries it to the crowd.

Hector tries to grab it but misses. "No, no, no!"

"Stay away from me!" Miguel says.

"No, ay." Hector scrambles for the photo, and Miguel takes the opportunity to run off. He doesn't look back, not even when he hears Hector calling, "Hey, chamaco! Where did you go? Chamaco! I'm sorry! Come back!"

CHAPTER 23

Miguel runs away as fast as he can. He sees de la Cruz's tower in the distance and heads for it. Dante's at his heels, whimpering. Then he starts barking, which is the last thing Miguel needs, especially with his family nearby.

"Dante, cállate!" he says.

But Dante is insistent. He tugs at Miguel's pants and tries to pull him back to the plaza. *He wants me to go back*, Miguel realizes. *He knows I want to leave, but instead of letting me go, he's pulling me in another direction—just like Hector. Just like my family!* He yanks his leg, but Dante's jaw is as strong as his family's rule against music. For a moment, Miguel and Dante are caught in a tug-of-war.

"No, Dante! Stop it! He can't help me!"

Miguel finally breaks free, but that doesn't stop Dante. The dog grabs Miguel's hoodie, and when Miguel tries to shake him off, the hoodie starts to slip off, revealing the arms of a living boy. Dante is even more insistent now. He will not stop barking.

"Dante, no, stop! Stop it! Leave me alone! You're supposed to be helping me! You're not a spirit guide. You're just a dumb dog. Now get out of here!"

Miguel forcefully yanks his hoodie away, and Dante shrinks back, rebuffed. But Miguel hasn't escaped—not yet. The noise catches the crowd's attention, and a dozen startled skeletons are shocked by Miguel's fleshy arms. He scrambles to cover himself, but it's too late. Everyone's pointing and calling even *more* attention to him.

"It's him!"

"It's that living boy!"

"I've heard about him. Look!"

"He's alive! The boy's alive!"

Miguel runs again. When he comes across a bench, he leaps over it. When he finds himself on a platform, he jumps down. He can see de la Cruz's tower in the distance and heads in that direction. He doesn't need Hector. He can get there on his own. But he needs to hurry before it's too late. He's already wasted too much time. He starts pumping his arms, palms flat because it's faster, but he only goes a few paces when an alebrije blocks his path, and it isn't something he can crawl under or jump over, because it's a giant jaguar! It has huge birdlike wings and talons instead of back claws. Miguel skids to a stop, nearly colliding with it.

"Aahh!" he cries, and when he sees the jaguar's fangs, he quakes with fear. But then he spots an even more terrifying sight—peeking over the jaguar's head is Mamá Imelda, and she's riding the creature like a cowboy on a horse!

"This nonsense ends now, Miguel! I am giving you my blessing and you are going home!"

"I don't want your blessing!"

He tries to bolt, but the giant alebrije grabs him with its talons and takes to the air. Miguel's legs still move, as if running, but they merely stir the air, because the ground is quickly falling away.

"Ahh . . . ahh . . . ahh! Let go of me! Put me down!"

All he hears is the steady beat of the alebrije's flapping wings. Miguel twists his body, but the talons are clamped tight. He punches at the creature's legs, but it doesn't flinch. Then he spots a line of papel picado, grabs it, and manages to wriggle free. Soon he's falling to the ground, and when he lands, he rolls a bit but quickly scrambles upright. Luckily, there's a narrow alley nearby. He bounds for it and hurries up a staircase.

"Miguel! Stop!" Mamá Imelda shouts. "Come back! Miguel!"

He glances back. The alley is too narrow for the jaguar, so Mamá Imelda's chasing him herself, holding up the hem of her skirt as she leaps up the stairs. At the top is an iron gate. Miguel slips his guitar between the bars and then squeezes through.

"I'm trying to save your life!" she says.

"You're ruining my life!"

"What?!"

She reaches the gate, but the bars are too close together. All she can do is put an arm through. Miguel backs away from her grasp.

"Music's the only thing that makes me happy. And you, you wanna take that away!" He takes a few steps up the stairs, distancing himself as much as possible. "You'll never understand."

He's about to sprint away when, to his amazement, Mamá Imelda sings in a beautiful, rich alto. The melancholy lyrics talk about a love that can never be lost.

Miguel stops and turns back, confused but also curious. "I thought you hated music."

"Oh, I love it," Mamá Imelda says. "I remember that feeling, when my husband would play, and I would sing, and nothing else mattered." She chuckles a bit, but then she frowns. "But when we had Coco, suddenly there was something in my life that mattered more than music. I wanted to put down roots. *He* . . . he wanted to play for the world." She pauses, lost in memory. "We each made a sacrifice to get what we wanted." She looks at Miguel. "Now *you* must make a choice."

"But I don't wanna pick sides! Why can't you be on *my* side?" Miguel gives her a moment to let this sink in, and then, his voice small, he continues, "That's what family's supposed to do. Support you. But you never will."

Miguel wipes the corner of his eye with the side of his palm, frustrated. When he glances at Mamá Imelda, she seems shocked at how hurt he feels, proof that she can't understand him. He doesn't waste any more time. He turns and continues his way up the stairs. De la Cruz's tower is not too far. At least *one* member of his family will understand what he's going through.

After Miguel disappears, Mamá Imelda reunites with Pepita, and they make their way back to the plaza. The contest is over. The audience has gone. The grass and marigolds are trampled flat, and the ground is littered with burnt-out sparklers, candy wrappers, straws, and Popsicle sticks. The BATTLE OF THE BANDS banner has come loose at one corner, hanging like the limp flag of a defeated country. The stage crew has removed the sound equipment, leaving behind a tangle of wires waiting to trip the next passerby.

"Look what music does," Mamá Imelda tells Pepita. "It turns a beautiful plaza into a pigsty."

Pepita roars in agreement.

"Mamá Imelda!" Papá Julio calls. He and the rest of the family are at the lost-and-found booth, waving her over.

When she reaches them, they pester her with questions.

"Where's Miguel?"

"Did you find him?"

"Did you send him home?"

"I found him," Mamá Imelda says, "but then I lost him again. He ran into a narrow alley and then . . . and then . . . Oh, never mind." She goes to a nearby bench and slumps onto it, full of despair.

The aunts rush to her side. "Tell us what happened," Tía Rosita says. "Is he hurt? Did he . . . did he turn into a skeleton?"

"Yes . . . no . . . I mean . . ." Mamá Imelda sighs deeply, unable to go on.

The whole family gathers around, and Tío Oscar puts a hand on her shoulder. "¿Qué pasó, hermana?"

"There was a moment," she explains, "I thought I could reach him. I . . . I sang."

The family gasps. They can't believe this.

"I wanted him to know that I once loved music, that I know its allure but that it's dangerous." She shakes her head. "But he won't listen. He's the most stubborn boy I've ever met. I don't know where he gets it from."

The Riveras glance at one another, all of them thinking that he's as stubborn as Mamá Imelda.

"At first I was mad because my picture wasn't on the ofrenda," she continues, "but now I don't care about that. I just want to send him home before it's too late! I don't know where he is or where to start looking. He could be anywhere!"

She sobs quietly and the family tries to console her. There are so many skyscrapers in the Land of the Dead, and each is exceedingly high. There's no way they can search all of them before sunrise.

They are at their lowest moment, about to give up hope, when they hear a dog barking. "Roo, roo, roooo!"

"Look!" Tía Victoria says, pointing. "It's that Xolo dog! *Miguel's* Xolo dog!"

Dante barges into the midst of their huddle, panting from running so hard. But he doesn't stay long. He trots a few steps away, then glances back. "Roo, roo!" he barks, urging them to follow.

"Do you know where he is?" Mamá Imelda asks as she rises from the bench.

Dante throws back his head and howls. It's the longest, loudest howl he's ever uttered, his own doggie version of a grito.

CHAPTER 24

After a long trek through strange streets, up escalators and stairways, on trolleys and sky cabs, Miguel finally reaches the foot of the hill with de la Cruz's tower, and he glances up to admire the glitz and glam. Vehicles from all eras pull into the circular drive—horse-drawn carriages with golden wheel spokes and velvet cushions, polished Model Ts, sporty convertibles, limousines, and party buses blaring dance tunes. Friendly hosts escort guests in tuxedos and formal evening gowns to a cliff rail that ascends the hill.

Miguel spies as a couple shows the security guard their fancy invitation. "Have a good time," the guard says.

"Oh, how exciting!" the woman exclaims.

Miguel wriggles between the next pair of guests, cutting to the front of the line. "Con permiso. De la Cruz coming through."

He had hoped to get by unnoticed, but the guard sees him. "Invitation?"

"It's okay," Miguel says. "I'm Ernesto de la Cruz's great-great-grandson." He points at his guitar and strikes de la Cruz's signature pose, but the guard is not convinced.

Next thing he knows, Miguel's being tossed out of the line. *Seriously?* he thinks. *Can't they see the resemblance?*

Just then, he spots Los Chachalacos unloading instruments from their van. They must have won the competition, and even though Miguel wanted that honor, he can't think of anyone more deserving. Los Chachalacos can really put on a show.

He approaches them. "Disculpen, señores."

"Hey, hey, guys," the band leader says. "It's Poco Loco!"

Miguel's chest swells with pride. He's flattered to learn they remember him and his performance.

The trumpet player says, "You were on fire tonight!"

"You too!" Miguel replies. "Hey, musician to musician, I need a favor."

They lean in to listen, and when Miguel explains his situation, especially the part about being de la Cruz's long lost great-great-grandson, they readily agree to help him sneak in.

"Lucky for you," the band leader says, "we got a sousa-phone."

Miguel realizes they want him to hide inside the large instrument, so he hands his guitar to one of the musicians. Then he crawls into the giant bell of the sousaphone, knees to chest so he can fit. One of the band members lifts it, groaning at the extra weight. Miguel's heart starts racing. He feels a little claustrophobic, but what choice does he have? He needs to reach the tower before he's all skin and bones, or rather, *skull* and bones. He wills himself to stay still and be silent.

Soon he feels himself being carried along, and then he hears the security guard, his voice a bit muffled. "Oooh, the competition winners! Congratulations, chicos!"

"Gracias! Gracias!" they say.

Then it gets quiet. Miguel guesses they are on the cliff rail. Once he feels movement again, the sousaphone player lowers the instrument so Miguel can crawl out.

"How are you so heavy, gordito?"

"I'm . . . big-boned?" Miguel says, crawling out and seeing that they are slowly going up the hill.

Finally, they reach the top, and the doors to the cliff rail open. The musicians give Miguel his guitar and file out. There before them is de la Cruz's lavish mansion!

"Whooaa!" Miguel is too awestruck to say more.

"Hey-hey!" the band leader says. "Enjoy the party, little músico!" They head to a side entrance so they can set up for their performance.

"Gracias!" Miguel calls after them. Then he turns to the mansion, feeling like a tiny housefly next to all this towering opulence. This is his great-great-grandfather's reward for having the courage to follow his dream. Miguel takes one more moment to admire it, and then he runs inside.

The party's bustling. Groups of skeletons mingle, laughing at jokes or pretending to be scandalized by gossip.

Then someone says, "Look, it's Ernesto!"

Miguel catches a glimpse of the back of someone who looks like de la Cruz heading deeper into the party. "De la Cruz," he whispers to himself, awed once again. He follows him up a staircase, but it's difficult to catch up with all the people around. They seem to part for de la Cruz, closing the gap after he passes and making it more difficult for Miguel to reach him.

"Señor de la Cruz!" he calls, elbowing his way through the room. "Pardon me. Señor de la Cruz! Señor de la—"

It's useless. Miguel's lost him in the crowd. Part of him wonders if he'll ever have a chance to get his great-great-grandfather's blessing.

He takes a minute to study his surroundings. He's in a huge circular hall with hundreds of guests, the heart of the party. Waiters carry silver platters with champagne flutes and hors d'oeuvres. There's a juggler, a magician, a flutist, a contortionist, and many other performers entertaining. And on the walls, long vertical banners serve as projector screens for clips of de la Cruz's movies.

On one banner, de la Cruz says, *"When you see your moment, you mustn't let it pass you by. You must seize it."*

On another, he says, *"This one has a wise spirit."*

On a third, he portrays a ghostly grandfather: *"You will pass down a song of your own, as I have done with you."*

Miguel's eyes are wide with astonishment. He's never been in such a fancy place before, but best of all, this hall is like a gigantic version of his secret hideout with all his de la Cruz memorabilia. How wonderful to be around so many others who appreciate de la Cruz as much as he does!

He takes it all in. Synchronized swimmers make formations in a guitar-shaped indoor pool, their swim caps as bright orange as marigolds. A DJ lays a soundtrack, a mariachi mash-up covering decades of the best groups and songs. Meanwhile, the film clips continue to loop on the banners.

"We're almost there, Dante," de la Cruz says in another film.

Miguel jumps to see above the crowd, and he thinks he spots him. "Señor de la Cruz! Señor de la—"

He stops, because his favorite clip from *Nuestra iglesia* is now playing.

Nun: *"But what can we do? It is hopeless. . . ."*

De la Cruz as the priest: *"You must have faith, Sister."*

Nun: *"Oh, but Padre, he will never listen."*

De la Cruz: *"He will listen . . . to music!"*

Yes, yes! Miguel tells himself. The passionate words have emboldened him. He knows what he has to do!

He climbs a banner to the landing of a grand staircase and stands above the crowd. Then, remembering his performance earlier, he takes a deep breath and throws out a grito as loud as he can! It echoes through the hall. The party guests turn, the performers freeze, and the DJ even mutes the music.

Now that Miguel has their attention, he strums his guitar. More guests turn, intrigued. A hush falls on the crowd, and soon Miguel's guitar is the only sound in the room. That is, until he starts singing. Of course, he sings a song by de la Cruz. It's an upbeat number that talks about music bringing joy and making everyone, even strangers, part of a family.

He continues to play and sing as he nervously steps toward the edge of the staircase landing. Now the crowd is parting for *him*. Little by little, he gets closer to de la Cruz, repeating the lines about music and family. He passes a movie screen where a clip features the same song, and for a brief moment, his and de la Cruz's voices overlap.

The crowd is captivated by his talent because he's singing with all his soul and heart. The world seems to fall away as Miguel continues to sing.

There's a sudden gasp from the crowd and then—*splash!* Miguel tumbles into the indoor pool!

Bubbles float around him. Disoriented, he can't tell which way is down and which is up. Plus, his arms are tangled in the guitar strap! He panics and his flailing only makes things worse. He can't believe he's drowning when he was so close to fulfilling his dream!

Suddenly, he feels a firm hand clasping his hoodie and pulling him up. Miguel breaks the surface. He's coughing, but he's alive. Someone drags him to the edge of the pool and lifts him out of the water. Then a voice asks, "Are you all right, niño?"

And when Miguel rubs the water from his eyes, he sees that the hero who jumped into the pool and rescued him is none other than . . . Ernesto de la Cruz!

CHAPTER 25

Miguel wipes his face with the sleeve of his jacket to get a better look, and that's when he realizes—the water from the pool has washed off his disguise! The crowd gasps and murmurs. De la Cruz's eyes go wide with shock.

"It's you," he says. "You, you are that boy, the one who came from the Land of the Living."

"You know about me?" Miguel asks.

"You're all anyone has been talking about! Why have you come here?"

"I'm Miguel. Your great-great-grandson."

The crowd murmurs again. A thread of excitement,

disbelief, and scandal runs through their voices, Miguel's announcement like a surprising twist in a telenovela.

"I . . . have a great-great-grandson?" de la Cruz says. At first he seems confused, but then pleasantly surprised.

Miguel nods and gives de la Cruz a moment to let the revelation sink in. Then he says, "I need your blessing so I can go back home and be a musician, just like you." He pauses because of the eavesdropping people, but he can't resist saying more. "The rest of our family, they wouldn't listen. But I . . . I hoped you would?"

The world seems to pause, waiting for de la Cruz's answer. Miguel holds his breath. And then, de la Cruz puts a hand on his shoulder. "My boy, with a talent like yours, how could I not listen?"

Miguel beams. He knew de la Cruz . . . no, Papá Ernesto . . . would understand! He thinks about all the times his family asked him to give up music, all the disappointment they felt when he dawdled or wasn't as involved with the shoemaking shop as he could have been, and all the tears he's cried. He's struggled so much, but now the struggle is over, because someone—the most important someone!—supports his dream.

De la Cruz embraces Miguel and then sweeps him onto his shoulders. He shows him off to the crowd and they erupt into wild applause. As they parade around, Miguel feels like a fútbol player who has just made the winning goal.

"I have a great-great-grandson!" de la Cruz announces, and the crowd roars again.

Giddy with excitement, de la Cruz barges into the mingling guests and interrupts their conversations with "This is my grandson! Would you like to meet my great-great-grandson? He's a musician like me!" And, of course, *everybody* wants to meet Miguel. He shakes hands, poses for pictures, even signs a few autographs. *So this is what it's like to be famous,* he thinks. *This is what it's like when the whole world loves you!*

They go to the garden, where de la Cruz introduces Miguel to some of Mexico's most famous celebrities, including Jorge Negrete and Pedro Infante! They ride horses to a field and interrupt a polo match so everyone can admire de la Cruz's great-great-grandson. Back in the mansion, de la Cruz tells everyone, "He's alive! And a musician to boot!" And Miguel shows off his fleshy features. "Dimple. No dimple," he says to a group in the parlor. "Dimple. No dimple." They're tickled, because skeletons don't have dimples. Some of the ladies delightedly poke Miguel's cheeks. He giggles, unable to believe that a few hours ago, the thought of being poked by skeletal fingers made him cringe.

To show off his entertaining talent, Miguel recites lines in sync with de la Cruz's characters on the screens.

"To our friendship!" Miguel says, changing his voice so that he sounds like the character Don Hidalgo. "I would move heaven and earth for you, mi amigo. ¡Salud!" He even pretends to take a sip and then to spit it out as another character, de la Cruz as a peasant, says, "Poison!" And when the characters start fighting, Miguel punches at the air in perfect unison with them.

"You know, I did all my own stunts," de la Cruz boasts.

Miguel can't imagine a more talented celebrity. His great-great-grandpa is amazing! He sings, acts, *and* does stunts!

"Sing! Sing!" the people beg.

So de la Cruz and Miguel start singing "Remember Me," and soon the whole crowd joins in. Everyone loops arms and sways to the music as they enter the ofrenda room. Once inside, the crowd oohs and aahs at the opulence. Miguel gasps. This isn't an ordinary ofrenda room. It's not a room at all. It's a warehouse filled with pan dulces, tequila, flowers, instruments, sombreros, trinkets, and demo tapes—all in massive piles that are several stories high. There's even a mountain of fan mail!

De la Cruz sweeps his arm across the room. "All of this came from my amazing fans in the Land of the Living! They leave me more offerings than I know what to do with!"

Miguel gawks. It's almost too much to absorb, like trying to see all the stars at once. The ofrenda room back home is small and shabby in comparison.

Miguel feels a sudden wave of regret, and de la Cruz notices, because he kneels down and looks into Miguel's eyes. "Hey, what's wrong? Is it too much? You look overwhelmed."

"No. It's all great," Miguel says.

"But . . . ?"

Miguel's not sure. Part of him remains impressed. Who *doesn't* dream of being loved like this, of living in a grand place with so many beautiful things? But another part of him . . .

"It's just . . . I've been looking up to you my whole

life. You're the guy who actually did it! But . . ." He takes a moment, worried he might offend his great-great-grandpa. "Did you ever regret it?" Miguel asks. "Choosing music over . . . everything else."

De la Cruz sighs. "It was hard," he admits. "Saying good-bye to Santa Cecilia. Heading off on my own."

"Leaving your family?"

"Sí. But I could not have done it differently. One cannot deny who one is meant to be. And you, my great-great-grandson, are meant to be a musician!"

The way de la Cruz speaks, with so much enthusiasm and conviction—it makes Miguel smile, and his chest swells with pride. For the first time in his life, he feels validated for being good at something he loves.

"You and I," de la Cruz continues, "we are artists, Miguel! We cannot belong to one family. The *world* is our family!"

Yes! Miguel thinks. *The world is our family.* He looks at the crowd. *All these people are my family, and as soon as I get the chance, I'm going to learn all their names!*

De la Cruz stands and gestures to the window. The sparkling city glows all around them. Miguel's never been so high before. He marvels at this view from the hilltop hacienda, how the people below look like ants bustling about. He wonders if one of those "ants" is his mamá Imelda, and he worries that she's going to turn up at the tower to ruin his chance of going home as a musician. But no. She would never come here, because she wants nothing to do with the man who left his family so many years ago.

Before Miguel can give this more thought, a firework booms and colors the sky.

"Oooh," de la Cruz says, giddy. "The fireworks have begun!"

The party guests move outside to watch the show while Miguel and de la Cruz head to the veranda overlooking the great hall. With the guests gone and the lights turned down, it's a dark, empty cavern. Flashes of color from outside cast creepy shadows across the walls. De la Cruz's films continue to play, but the words seem rehearsed and insincere, probably because the speakers need an adjustment after looping through the audio clips all evening.

They descend the staircase into the emptied hall, Miguel happy to finally have a moment alone with his great-great-grandfather.

"Soon the party will move across town for my Sunrise Spectacular," de la Cruz says. Then he gasps, his voice full of excitement. "Miguel, you must come to the show! You will be my guest of honor!"

"You mean it?"

"Of course, my boy!"

Miguel's chest swells again, and his eyes light up. He's going to be the guest of honor at the Sunrise Spectacular—the capstone event for the Land of the Dead's holiday celebration!

He stops himself. Wait a minute. The *Sunrise* Spectacular. When his skeletal transformation will be complete!

Miguel lifts his shirt and reveals his rib cage. "I can't. I have to get home before sunrise."

De la Cruz frowns at Miguel's transformation. "Ooey, I really do need to get you home," he says. He searches for a marigold petal and plucks one from a vase. Then he stands before Miguel. "It has been an honor. I am sorry to see you go, Miguel. I hope you die very soon." He catches himself, and chuckling, he says, "You know what I mean."

Miguel nods and then he straightens, ready for his blessing.

"Miguel," de la Cruz begins, "I give you my bles—"

Before he can utter another syllable, a voice calls out from the darkness. "We had a deal, chamaco!"

CHAPTER 26

Hector can't believe it. He almost missed his chance to cross the Marigold Bridge!

"Who are you?" Ernesto calls out. "What is the meaning of this?" Hector steps from the shadows, and Ernesto looks delighted. "Oh, Frida!" he says, because Hector's in costume again. "I thought you couldn't make it."

But Hector addresses Miguel instead. "You said you'd take back my photo. You promised."

When Hector throws off the wig and the dress, Miguel backs into de la Cruz, who puts his hands defensively on Miguel's shoulders.

"You know this, uh . . . man?"

"I just met him tonight," Miguel says. "He told me he knew you."

Hector steps forward, holding the photo. He has only one mission—to get it to an ofrenda before it's too late. "Please, Miguel, put my photo up."

He pushes it toward Miguel's hands, but Ernesto intercepts, glancing at the picture and then at the gray, faded skeleton before him. Recognition slowly creeps onto his face, and for a moment, Hector's ashamed to be so tattered and frail.

"My friend," Ernesto says, "you're . . . you're being forgotten."

"And whose fault is that?" Hector asks as bitter memories come flooding in.

"Hector, please."

"Those were *my* songs you took. *My* songs that made *you* famous."

"W-What?" Miguel stutters.

"If I'm being forgotten," Hector continues, "it's because *you* never told anyone that I wrote them."

"That's crazy," Miguel says. "De la Cruz wrote all his own songs."

Hector shakes his head. The entire world has been fooled all these years, and this poor kid has spent his life idolizing a con man. He hates to come between Miguel and his great-great-grandfather, but isn't it better for the boy to know the truth?

"You wanna tell him, or should I?" he asks Ernesto.

"Hector, I never meant to take credit." Ernesto pauses, remembering. "We made a great team, but . . . you died, and . . . I . . . I only sang your songs because I wanted to keep a part of you alive."

"Oh, how generous," Hector says sarcastically.

"You really did play together?" Miguel asks.

Hector sighs. "Look," he says, "I don't want to fight about it, Ernesto. I just want you to make it right. Miguel can put my photo up—"

"Hector . . ."

"And I can cross over the bridge. I can see my girl."

Instead of answering, Ernesto looks at the photo, deliberating. *What's there to think about?* Hector wonders. As far as he's concerned, Ernesto can keep the fame, the parties, and the shining, bright tower. All he wants is a chance to visit the Land of the Living. Little by little, his clothes are getting more tattered and his bones more brittle. If he doesn't get his picture on an ofrenda tonight, he'll disappear just like Chicharrón.

"Ernesto," Hector says, keeping his voice calm because he really doesn't want to fight, "remember what you told me the night I left?"

"That was a long time ago."

"We drank together and you told me you would move heaven and earth for your amigo. Well, I'm asking you to now."

"Heaven and earth?" Miguel repeats. "Like in the movie?"

"What?" Hector asks. He can't believe how obsessed

people are with movies. There weren't many films when he was alive, so he never bothered to watch them after he died. He couldn't name a single famous movie, so he doesn't know what Miguel's talking about.

"That's Don Hidalgo's toast," Miguel explains. "In the movie *El camino a casa*."

"I'm talking about my real life, Miguel."

"No, it's in there. Look."

Miguel points to a movie clip being projected across the room. Up till now, Hector hasn't paid attention to the screens. But there he is—Ernesto, dressed as a peasant and speaking to a handsome man, who must be Don Hidalgo, and who's holding up a glass.

"Never were truer words spoken," Don Hidalgo says. *"This calls for a toast! To our friendship! I would move heaven and earth for you, mi amigo."*

"But in the movie," Miguel explains, "Don Hidalgo poisons the drink . . ." His voice trails off for a second. Hector wonders what he's thinking about. "Don Hidalgo poisons the drink," Miguel continues, "so he can steal de la Cruz's farm."

"¡Salúd!" Don Hidalgo says.

Hector watches as the characters each take a drink, as Ernesto, acting, spits and utters, *"Poison!"*

Wait a minute! Wait a minute! Hector's brain is screaming. *This is all too familiar!*

"That night," he says to Ernesto. "The night I left. We'd been performing on the road for months. I got homesick, and I packed up my songs. . . ."

CHAPTER 27

The past floods back. Hector and Ernesto had toured all over Mexico, in dozens of cities—Toluca, San Luis Potosí, Monterrey, and every little town in between. Every night, they were in a new location. They stayed in different hotels, but since all the rooms looked the same, Hector got confused. Each morning, he'd wake up wondering where he was. Which city this time?

But it didn't matter—at first, because he was there to do something he loved, but later, because it was the same routine every time. At every stop, he and Ernesto posted flyers and went to all the plazas and cantinas to tell people about their show. Sometimes they had a large audience, but most times, a modest one. It was the same amount of work regardless of who showed up. Hector didn't care. He was as happy alone as he was in front of a crowd as long as he could play his songs. But Ernesto was another story. Without a large audience, he performed half-heartedly. He just couldn't get into the music. It amazed Hector to see his friend so charming and energetic one day but gloomy and tired the next, and that's when Hector realized that popularity, not music, fed Ernesto's soul.

Hector soon regretted his decision to go on the road. He thought touring would inspire him, give him material for more music. He thought it would help him make a living while doing something he loved. But he didn't need to be on the road to play his songs. The people in his hometown always needed music for weddings, parties, holidays, and bailes, or for no special reason at all.

So one night, when they were in Mexico City, Hector made a decision. He couldn't be on the road anymore. How he longed to sleep in his own bed again, to be near friends and family. Yes, Ernesto was his best friend, but it had been a mistake to join him. So Hector threw his songbook in his suitcase and grabbed his guitar. He was ready to leave, but his friend refused to let him go.

"You wanna give up now?" Ernesto said. "When we're this close to reaching our dream?"

"This was *your* dream," Hector argued. "You'll manage."

When he headed toward the door, Ernesto grabbed him by the suitcase, but Hector pulled away.

"I can't do this without your songs," Ernesto pleaded.

"I'm going home," Hector said, adamant. "Hate me if you want, but my mind is made up."

Ernesto fumed, dark anger crossing his face. Hector worried he'd lose his friend forever. Even though they had different ambitions, they both still loved music. Plus, they had grown up together, like primos. Hector couldn't remember a time when Ernesto wasn't around. The last thing he wanted was to anger his best friend. He was about to explain this when Ernesto brushed aside his dark mood and became cheerful again.

"Oh, I could never hate you," Ernesto said, playfully punching Hector's shoulder. "If you must go, then I'm . . . I'm sending you off with a toast!"

Ernesto poured a couple of drinks, and Hector gladly took the glass he was offered. More than anything, he wanted to end this adventure in peace and with their friendship intact.

"To our friendship!" Ernesto said, raising his glass. "I would move heaven and earth for you, mi amigo. ¡Salud!"

Then they both took a sip.

After Hector emptied his glass, he grabbed his suitcase and guitar. "It's time," he announced. "I must go."

"I'll walk to the train station with you," Ernesto said.

Hector was glad for the company. It was like the old days again. On the way to the station, they joked about their adventures, and every time they laughed, they roused the sleeping dogs, making them bark. But it was late, the streets empty. No one glanced out a window or switched on a porch light, so the streets remained dark.

Suddenly, Hector's suitcase and guitar became very heavy. He stumbled, and Ernesto reached out to steady him and took the suitcase to lighten the load.

"Are you okay?" he asked.

Hector grabbed his stomach. "Ay," he moaned. "It must be something I ate."

"Maybe it was the chorizo," Ernesto said.

Hector moaned even louder, then doubled over from the pain. *I have food poisoning,* he wanted to say. He needed a doctor. He *had* to call for a doctor! But before he could utter a word, he collapsed.

And that is the last thing he remembers.

CHAPTER 28

"**Later,** I woke up dead," Hector says, the realization coming to him. "It wasn't the chorizo after all. It was the drink. You poisoned me—just like the character in the film."

"You're confusing movies with reality," Ernesto says, his arms extended.

"All this time I thought it was just bad luck." Hector clenches his jaw as he imagines the scene after his collapse. Ernesto must have taken his songbook. That's what happened—he's sure of it now. "I never thought that you might have . . ." Now he clenches his jaw *and* his fists. "That you . . ."

He can't finish. Anger and betrayal surge through him. He bounds at Ernesto, tackling him to the ground.

"Hector!" Miguel shouts.

But Hector ignores him. He's too angry. "How could you?!"

"Security! Security!" Ernesto cries as he and Hector scuffle on the floor.

"You took everything away from me!"

They wrestle. Every time they roll, Hector worries that his bones will shatter in all directions and then turn to dust, but his anger gives him strength. He's about to clamp a chokehold when the security guards rush in. Hector tries to fight them off, but it's no use. He's outnumbered, and in his weakened condition, he has no chance.

"You rat!" he yells when they pull him away.

Ernesto stands and coolly brushes himself off. "Have him taken care of. He's not well."

"You rat!" Hector yells again as the guards drag him through the doorway. "I just wanted to go back home!"

He wanted to go back home that night in Mexico City, and he wants to go home right now. He has to get back to his girl.

Hector glances back, once again seeing the opportunity slip from his hands. "No! No! Nooo!"

When the doors shut, Miguel can no longer hear Hector's cries, and he feels caught between the man he's only recently gotten to know, Hector, and his great-great-grandfather, de la Cruz, someone he's known his whole life—or rather, someone he's known *about*.

Miguel has never felt so torn. De la Cruz is the reason he loves music. Besides, Hector's a con man! Or maybe he's not. Maybe he's a friend. *I'm related to a great musician,* Miguel assures himself. *No, I'm related to a . . .*

De la Cruz interrupts his thoughts. "I apologize," he says. "Where were we?"

"You were going to give me your blessing."

"Yes. Uh . . . sí." De la Cruz plucks another marigold petal from the vase, but then he hesitates. "Miguel, my reputation. It is very important to me. I would hate to have you think . . ."

"That you murdered Hector?" Miguel's words come out before he can stop himself.

"You don't think that. Do you?"

"I . . . no. Everyone knows you're the . . . the good guy."

But is he? Miguel asks himself, thinking of the ofrenda room with its giant piles of gifts. De la Cruz's fans leave him more offerings than he knows what to do with. Isn't that what he said? So why doesn't de la Cruz share any of it? Miguel thinks of Shantytown. Lots of people in the Land of the Dead have nothing. Surely he can spare a gift? And what about that pile of letters? Most of them were still in sealed envelopes. Had he read *any* of them?

What about *Miguel's* offerings? Once he left a poem, thinking de la Cruz could put it to music. Another time he left a commemorative coffee mug with de la Cruz's face on it, using his allowance for the purchase. But did his great-great-grandfather ever notice or care?

Miguel looks at de la Cruz's face. A dark shadow crosses over it, and the eyes are suddenly sinister. Instead of preparing for the blessing, de la Cruz is stuffing Hector's photo into his pocket.

"Papá Ernesto?" Miguel says. "My blessing?"

In response, de la Cruz's smile is replaced with a sneer. He crumples the marigold petal and shouts, "Security!" His guards appear immediately. "Take care of Miguel," he instructs. "He'll be extending his stay."

They roughly grab him by the shoulders. Miguel has never felt more betrayed. This is worse than the moment his family denied his dream. De la Cruz is denying Miguel his life!

"What?!" Miguel cries. "But I'm your family!"

"And Hector was my best friend," de la Cruz says coldly.

Miguel gulps and goes pale. He doesn't want to believe it, but it's true. "You *did* murder him!"

"Success doesn't come for free, Miguel." De la Cruz sounds as though he thinks he's giving good advice. "You have to be willing to do whatever it takes—to seize your moment. I know you understand."

The guards take Miguel away, and like Hector, he cries out, "No! No!"

But it's no use. They have their orders and they obey. They drag him through the exit, to the back of de la Cruz's mansion.

"Let go!" Miguel shouts as he struggles to get away.

And they *do* let go—right into a cenote, an inescapable sinkhole behind the estate. Miguel falls four stories down!

"No! Ahhhh!" He splashes into a pool. It isn't very deep. He can feel the muddy bottom, but he still has to paddle his way to an island of stone at the center.

"Help!" he cries, cupping his hands around his mouth to make a megaphone. "Can anyone hear me? I wanna go home! I need to go . . ." His voice bounces off the walls, mocking him, and Miguel collapses in defeat. "I need to go home," he whimpers. Even his tiny voice echoes in the rocky chamber.

He can see the sky in the opening far above, but the walls of the cenote are tall, steep, and slippery with damp algae. All he hears is an occasional plop of water. How will he ever escape? To make matters worse, his soaked hoodie sags off, and instead of skin and muscle, he sees the ball and socket of a bony shoulder haloed by a soft glow. His transformation is almost complete. Morning is just around the corner, and even if he manages to escape the cenote, he will never escape the Land of the Dead.

Miguel groans and curls into himself. He's never felt more alone.

But then, mixed with the sound of plopping water, he hears footsteps. When he turns toward the noise, he sees a familiar face! Hector is stumbling from the darkness. The poor hombre's clothes are even more tattered, and he's got cracks and scuff marks on his bones from being manhandled by the guards.

"Hector?"

"Kid?"

"Oh, Hector!"

They run to each other, sloshing through the water, and then they embrace. They might be in a dire situation, but at least they have each other.

"You were right," Miguel rambles. "I should have gone back to my family."

"Hey, hey, hey," Hector soothes.

"They told me not to be like de la Cruz, but I didn't listen."

"It's okay."

Miguel thinks about the last thing he said to his family and cringes with shame. "I told them I didn't care if they remembered me. I didn't care if I was on their stupid ofrenda." What if he never gets a chance to make it right?

He's shaking with regret and anger, so Hector holds him to his chest.

"Hey, chamaco. It's okay. It's okay."

"I told them I didn't care," Miguel sobs. He backs away, wipes his tears, and takes a few calming breaths, but he still feels hopeless.

Suddenly, a golden flicker flutters through Hector's bones, and he falls to his knees. Hector grabs his gut like someone getting punched. "Hhuuh!" he groans.

"Hector!"

"She's . . . forgetting me."

"Who?" Miguel asks.

"My daughter," Hector says.

"She's the reason you wanted to cross the bridge?"

"I just wanted to see her again." Hector shakes his head with his own regret. "I never should have left Santa Cecilia. Ernesto convinced me that my 'big moment' was waiting for me far away from home, but . . . my family . . . *they* were my big moment. I wish I could apologize. I wish I could tell her that her papá was trying to come home. That he loved her so much." He closes his eyes. "My Coco . . ."

A chill runs through Miguel. "Coco?" It could be a coincidence, but what are the odds that Hector would know someone named Coco, someone who is forgetting things, just like Miguel's great-grandmother? He reaches into his hoodie and looks at the photo of Imelda, Coco, and the faceless musician. Then he shows it to Hector, who's confused, like he's seen a ghost.

"Where . . . where did you get this?"

"That's my mamá Coco," Miguel explains. "That's my mamá Imelda." He points at the man. "Is that you?"

A glimmer of recognition crosses Hector's face. "We're . . . family?"

Miguel is shocked. He looks at his true great-great-grandpa, and yes, the cheekbones and the chin are familiar. They remind him of . . . of Mamá Coco! How could he have been so blind? His great-great-grandfather was beside him the entire time! He compares Hector and de la Cruz. *Hector's* the one who gave advice about music, while de la Cruz gave advice about fame. Hector taught him about playing a song from the heart; de la Cruz was just concerned about his reputation. Yes, everything makes sense now. *I'm related to a real musician,* Miguel thinks, realizing for the first time that being a *real* musician is not necessarily the same thing as being a *famous* one.

Hector gently touches Miguel's cheek as if to confirm that the boy is real, and then he touches the image of baby Coco. "I always hoped I'd see her again," he says with a saddened voice. "That she'd miss me . . . maybe put up my photo. But it never happened. And you know the worst part?"

Miguel shakes his head.

"Even if I never got to see Coco in the living world, I thought at least one day I'd see her here. Give her the biggest hug." His dreamy voice gets sad again. "But she's the last person who remembers me. The moment she's gone from the living world . . ."

"You disappear from this one," Miguel finishes. "You'll never get to see her."

"Never again."

Music is why Hector and Miguel left their family. Now, here they are, both about to disappear—Hector from the Land of the Dead and Miguel from the Land of the Living. And Miguel knows that they both wish, more than anything, that they could reunite with their loved ones, no matter what.

Hector starts to speak again. "Listen, chamaco, when I used to play for my family—I've never been so happy." He gets a faraway look in his eyes. "You know, I wrote Coco a song once. We used to sing it every night at the same time.

No matter how far apart we were. What I wouldn't give to sing it to her one last time."

Hector begins to sing softly. It is the famous "Remember Me," but a much sincerer version. Miguel remembers Hector's advice about singing from the heart and dedicating your songs to someone special. *He's singing to Coco,* Miguel realizes. *No wonder the song is so famous. No wonder it's touched so many hearts. It's filled with the secret ingredient—love.*

As Hector sings, Miguel imagines a young Mamá Coco singing along. The lyrics, particularly the parts about remembering someone when they are far away, about knowing they are still with you, have a new meaning now.

Hector sighs heavily. "He stole my songs," he says about de la Cruz. "He stole my guitar. He stole *everything* from me."

Miguel is outraged. "We can't let him get away with this! *You* should be the one the world remembers, not de la Cruz."

"I didn't write 'Remember Me' for the world. I wrote it for Coco. I'm a pretty sorry excuse for a great-great-grandpa."

"Are you kidding?" Miguel says, trying to lighten the mood. "A minute ago, I thought I was related to a murderer. You're a total upgrade."

Hector doesn't smile, and it breaks Miguel's heart to see his great-great-grandpa so depressed. Especially because he understands what it's like to feel alone. But Miguel is *not* alone, and neither is Hector. They have each other. More than that, they have a love for music *and* for family.

"My whole life," Miguel says, "there's been something

inside me, something that made me different, and I never knew where it came from." He puts a hand on Hector's shoulder. "But now I know. It comes from *you*. I'm proud we're family!" He looks up at the hole in the cenote and shouts, "I'm proud to be his family! Trrrrrai-hay-hay-hay-haaay!"

Hector perks up and follows with his own grito: "Trrrrrraaaaai-haaai-haaaaay!"

He rolls his *r*'s and extends his *a*'s and puts every drop of his fading energy into it. Miguel tries to outdo him, but every time, Hector comes back with a stronger, more defiant grito. They trade off shouts until the cenote echoes with the sound! Soon the echoes and gritos are indistinguishable. They're in a drum of their own making, the sound waves booming through their bones. For a moment, Hector seems more alive, but then he's panting, exhausted. While he tries to catch his breath, the echoes fade, and the cenote gets silent again. In spite of their victorious cries, they are still stuck. There's no escape from this situation. They can't shout their way to freedom.

Miguel's shoulders droop. He's got nothing left, but then he hears something in the distance. He turns his head, cups his ear. It's a familiar sound—a wonderfully familiar sound, for he hears a distant "Rooo-rooo-roooooooo!"

Miguel and Hector look up.

"Dante?" Miguel calls.

"Roooooo-roo-roo-rooo!" It's closer now. And then—it's there! From the upper edge of the cenote, Dante peeks down.

"Dante!" Miguel laughs. "It's Dante!!"

The little dog pants and wags his tail happily. Then, from behind him, two more figures peek down—Mamá Imelda and Pepita. When Miguel and Mamá Imelda catch each other's eyes, they laugh with joy. Pepita roars happily, the sound shaking the cavern.

Then Hector says, "Imelda! You still look good."

Miguel realizes this is the first time they've seen each other in person in many years. When Mamá Imelda notices Hector, her joyous face looks surprised and then turns cold, and Miguel has to wonder, *Will she ever forgive him?*

CHAPTER 29

There's no time for explanations or apologies. It's almost sunrise, and Miguel must go home. Pepita glides into the cenote, landing on the rocky island and letting Hector and Miguel climb onto her back, joining Mamá Imelda and Dante. Then the graceful alebrije rises out of the cenote, ascending above the clouds where the tallest skyscrapers pierce through.

Miguel's hood falls off and his hair flaps in the wind, just like Dante's goofy tongue. Miguel pets him and suddenly remembers that it was Dante who revealed the hidden picture on the ofrenda, Dante who found Hector in the security office when Miguel first ran away, and Dante who urged Miguel to stay with Hector after the Battle of the Bands.

"Dante," Miguel says, hugging the dog fiercely, "you *knew* he was my papá Hector the whole time! You were trying to bring us together. You are a real spirit guide!" He switches to his doggie-praising voice. "Who's a good spirit guide? You are!"

Dante smiles dumbly, and then, right before Miguel's eyes, neon patterns spread outward from the dog's paws. His tongue goes green, his nose turns yellow, and his body becomes a beautiful mosaic of red, blue, and pink!

"Whoa!" Miguel says as a pair of little wings sprout on Dante's back. Dante spreads and flaps them as if to see if they're sky-worthy. Then he jumps off Pepita's back, but instead of flying . . . he plummets beneath the clouds!

"Dante!" Miguel cries, worried for his friend. A few seconds later, the little dog is back up, flapping goofily and barking loudly. Instead of the smooth, even flight of Pepita, Dante dips down and zigzags like an erratic butterfly, but it doesn't matter—he's a full-blown alebrije!

Finally, Pepita starts to descend. Miguel peeks over her shoulder and spots a small plaza with a group of people waving at them. It's the rest of his family! He has never felt so happy to see his relatives, and he can't wait to be reunited with his living family in Santa Cecilia.

As they get closer, Papá Julio jumps up and down excitedly, his head springing off and on like the ball on a paddle toy. "Look, there they are!" he says.

Pepita lands, and the Riveras surround her, everyone talking at the same time.

"Miguel!"

"Miguelito!"

"Ay, gracias!"

"It's Miguel! He's all right!"

"Oh, thank goodness!"

Hector dismounts first. He raises his arm to help Imelda, but she responds with a withering stare and climbs down on her own. Then Miguel gets down, all the while looking up at Dante, who's circling above, not quite sure how to land.

"C'mon, Dante," Miguel says, "you can do it!"

Dante comes in for a landing but loses his balance and skids on his rump before coming to a stop. He shakes himself off and trots over to Miguel, who hugs him again. Dante responds with a sloppy lick.

Now that they're on firm ground, Mamá Imelda folds Miguel into a tight hug. "M'ijo," she says, "I was so worried! Thank goodness we found you in time!" She touches his shoulders and hands to make sure he's all there. Then she releases him and turns her attention to Hector, who is sheepishly holding his hat. "And *you*!" she scolds, pointing and angrily poking him. "Must I always clean up your messes?!"

"Imelda—" Hector says, but she won't hear it.

"Seducing him with promises of . . . of music and fame!"

"Mamá Imelda—" Miguel starts, because he wants to defend Hector, but he's shut down, too.

"I spent my whole life trying to protect my family from

your mistakes, and *he*," Mamá Imelda points at Miguel for emphasis, "spends five minutes with you and I have to fish him out of a sinkhole!"

Miguel can't take it anymore. Poor Hector has been blamed his whole life for something he didn't do. Before Mamá Imelda can say more, he steps between them.

"It's my fault," Miguel says. "I wasn't in the cenote because of Hector. He was in there because of *me*. He was just trying to get me home. I didn't wanna listen, but he was right—nothing is more important than family."

The Riveras nod, for this has always been their philosophy, but Mamá Imelda seems shocked to hear that Hector believes this, too.

Before she can comment, Tía Rosita says, "But why were you in the cenote in the first place? And why were you in Shantytown? And how did you slip away from the plaza before we saw you?"

"We don't have time for all these questions," Tía Victoria says.

Tío Oscar agrees. "That's right. It's time to send Miguel home, so he can get back to his family and we can get back to poking out eyes."

Miguel flinches, imagining a bowl of eyeballs.

His tíos notice. "Not the eyes you see with," Tío Oscar says.

"Or the windows to the soul," adds Tío Felipe.

"Or the eye of a potato."

"Of a storm."

"Of a—"

"Okay, okay," Miguel laughs. "You mean eyelets for shoe-laces."

Everyone nods as if this were the most obvious thing.

Then Miguel turns to Mamá Imelda. "I'm ready to accept your blessing, and your conditions. But first, I need to find de la Cruz to get Hector's photo."

"What?" Mamá Imelda sounds scandalized.

"So he can see Coco again," Miguel explains. "Hector should be on our ofrenda. He's part of our family."

"He left his family!"

"He tried to go home to you and Coco, but de la Cruz murdered him!"

The Riveras gasp, and Mamá Imelda takes a step back, startled. Then she looks to Hector as if seeking confirmation.

"It's true, Imelda."

Her face softens a bit, her eyes full of pity and regret—but then she steels herself. "So what if it's true? That changes things? You leave me alone with a child to raise, and I'm just supposed to forgive you?"

"Imelda, I—" Before Hector can finish, his body shimmers, leaving him winded. Imelda gasps. "I'm running out of time," Hector says weakly.

For a minute, Mamá Imelda looks at him, confused. Then she figures out what's happening. "It's Coco. She's forgetting you."

"You don't have to forgive him," Miguel says, his voice urgent. "But we shouldn't *forget* him."

Mamá Imelda sighs. Miguel can hear her sadness. "Oh, Hector," she says, "I wanted to forget you. I wanted Coco to forget you, too, but . . ."

"This is my fault . . . not yours," Hector says. "I'm sorry, Imelda."

Mamá Imelda looks as torn as Miguel feels. He can only guess how difficult it must be to put so many years of bitterness aside.

Instead of formally accepting Hector's apology, Mamá Imelda turns to Miguel. "If we help you get his photo . . . you will return home? No more music?"

Miguel nods. "Family comes first."

She considers this a moment. Then she addresses Hector. "I . . . I don't forgive you. But I will help you."

Miguel smiles. It isn't a true reconciliation; the wound runs deep, but at least it's a start.

"So how do we get to de la Cruz?" Mamá Imelda asks Miguel.

He furrows his brow, thinking. "I might know a way. . . ."

CHAPTER 30

The Sunrise Spectacular is about

to begin. Hundreds of skeletons have gathered in a huge coliseum, located in one of the tallest skyscrapers in the Land of the Dead. Fireworks explode above like colorful lightning, and their loud booms mix with the excited murmurs of the crowd. The attendees study the aisle and row numbers printed on their tickets and make their way up and down the stairs, looking for their seats. Soon, nearly everyone has settled in, so the stragglers have to say "perdóname" a dozen times as they trip and stumble past knees and shoulders in the crowded rows. They talk excitedly, predicting what they'll see, which songs they'll hear, and as they wait, they enjoy offerings from the Land of the Living, the sodas and dulces their loved ones have left behind.

Finally, the moment they've been waiting for! Symphonic music comes on, and everyone hushes to watch the show. A spotlight shines upon a giant papaya and then flits about the stage, teasing the audience, for they expect Ernesto de la Cruz at any moment. Suddenly, the papaya ignites, and the audience gasps in delight! Smoke rises, and for a moment, the round bowl of the coliseum seems like a cauldron. As the shell of the papaya burns away, dancers from within unfurl themselves. The audience oohs and aahs when the Frida Kahlo clones are revealed—short, tall, plump, skinny, male, female—they seem to be caricatures of the famous artist, and all are dancing nonsensically.

Finally, a giant cactus is illuminated. It is Frida, the cactus mother! One by one, the dancers slink into the cactus, but eight familiar-looking dancers—the dead Riveras and Miguel—inch their way out of the spotlight and into the wings of the stage. Waiting for them is Frida Kahlo—the *real* Frida. The whole family is starstruck.

"Good luck, muchacho," Frida says, for she has helped them sneak into the coliseum.

"Gracias, Frida!" Miguel says, and when she exits, the family waves goodbye.

After a moment to catch their breath from the dancing and excitement of meeting a celebrity, Mamá Imelda says, "Now let's get out of these contraptions."

Tío Oscar lifts his skirt, revealing Dante, who's been

hiding underneath. Miguel rips off his unibrow and cries out, "Ow!" Hector manages to remove the entire costume in one swift move, which seems to irritate Mamá Imelda because she's tangled in her dress and because it's . . . well . . . it's Hector.

"Here, let me help you," he offers.

She turns a cold shoulder. "Don't touch me."

His shoulders droop. A guilty look flashes across Mamá Imelda's face, but only for a tiny second.

Then Papá Julio removes his pumps and slips his feet back into his western boots. "So how did I do?" he wants to know. "Did I make a convincing Frida?"

"*Very* convincing," Miguel says, "except that you're a lot older."

"And shorter," Tía Victoria adds, "less curvy, and a little too squat."

💀💀💀💀

After they're free of their costumes, Mamá Imelda gathers everyone in a huddle. When Hector squeezes into the spot beside her, she shuffles over to get away from him, using her twin hermanos as a shield.

After she reviews the plan, Miguel asks, "Everyone clear?"

Tía Victoria says, "Find Hector's photo."

"Give it to Miguel," Papá Julio adds.

"Send Miguel home," Mamá Imelda concludes.

When Hector asks if they have their marigolds, each of them holds up a petal. This means that whoever finds the photo can send Miguel home. They have a moment of quiet reflection and then tiptoe out, Mamá Imelda leading the way. "Now we just have to find de la Cruz," she says, wondering how they will ever find him in the maze of corridors backstage.

Then she turns the corner and . . . nearly bumps into Ernesto de la Cruz!

"Yes?" he says.

"Ah!" Mamá Imelda shrieks.

The family behind her freezes in their tracks and stays hidden. She must face him alone.

She should be afraid of him after learning about the terrible things he's done to her family, but instead, her anger begins to swell.

"Don't I know you?" de la Cruz says.

Instead of answering yes or no, Mamá Imelda grabs a huarache from her apron pocket and slaps him with all her might!

"That's for murdering the love of my life!" she shouts.

De la Cruz rubs his cheek, disoriented. "What the . . . ? Who the . . . ?"

Then Hector leaps out. "She's talking about me!" he says, then to her, "I'm the love of your life?"

"I don't know," Mamá Imelda says. "I'm still angry at you."

"Hector," de la Cruz says, recovering, "how did you—"

Before he can say more, Mamá Imelda slaps him again. "And that's for trying to murder my grandson!"

"Grandson?"

Now Miguel leaps out of the corridor, and when de la Cruz sees the three of them, he puts the pieces together.

"You!" he gasps. "Wait. You're related to Hector?"

Instead of answering, Miguel points to de la Cruz's pocket. "The photo!" he says.

The rest of the Riveras rush out, and de la Cruz's eyes widen when he sees them. *He's outnumbered,* Mamá Imelda realizes, satisfied. *Surely he'll surrender the photo without a fight.* But they aren't that lucky. De la Cruz bolts away.

"After him!" Mamá Imelda charges.

They chase him through dark corridors, up stairwells, and into mess halls and equipment storage areas—circling the coliseum like horses circling a corral. When they reach an intersection of hallways, they lose him momentarily, and when they spot him again, he's running toward the stage. They waste no time and sprint in pursuit.

"Security!" de la Cruz cries. "Ayúdame!"

The family floods out onto the stage, Hector running beside Imelda. He says, "You said 'love of your life.'"

"I don't know *what* I said!"

"That's what I heard," Miguel chuckles from behind.

She couldn't be more embarrassed. "Can we focus on the matter at hand?"

Before the family can reach de la Cruz, the guards respond to his call. They're quick to engage, and a brawl ensues. But the family will not be stopped. Papá Julio knocks down a guard with a well-placed karate kick. Tío Felipe pulls Oscar's arms off and swings them like bolas to trip a few more guards, and Oscar pounces on them, keeping them pinned down. But de la Cruz is still on the loose.

"Places, señor, you're on in thirty seconds!" a stagehand says.

De la Cruz shoves him aside. While the security guards wrestle with the Riveras, Mamá Imelda sees an opening. She sprints forward and gets close enough to grab Hector's photo from de la Cruz's pocket. He scuffles with her to get it back, slapping at her arms as she juggles it back and forth, and then grabbing her apron, refusing to let go. *This man has no respect for women!* she thinks. Luckily, she manages to hold him off, and then Miguel gets through the guards and tackles de la Cruz to the ground, making him lose his grip. Mamá Imelda tumbles backward, photo still in hand.

"Miguel!" she calls. "I have it!"

He turns toward her, but before he can grab the photo the guards recover and start chasing him. Then it's too late. Miguel's out of reach because, suddenly, Mamá Imelda is rising into the air! That's when she realizes she's on de la Cruz's rising platform.

She peeks over the edge. As the platform rises, stairs unfold along the edges, and de la Cruz is not far behind!

"Miguel!" she calls.

And then she spots him, still struggling with a guard. He gets smaller and smaller as the platform goes higher and higher. She's nearly in a panic. How will she deliver the photo?

She's about to lose all hope when Dante flies in. After a

few clumsy flybys, he manages to knock off the head of the guard holding Miguel.

Miguel breaks free, shouting to the family, "Hurry, come on!" And while the uncles and Papá Julio block the guards, Miguel, Hector, and his aunts run up to the platform, right behind de la Cruz.

Meanwhile, the show must go on. Mamá Imelda hears the emcee's voice. "Ladies and gentlemen. The one, the only . . . Ernesto de la Cruz!"

Suddenly, a spotlight falls on Mamá Imelda and neon letters blast brightly behind her, spelling out ERNESTO! The audience bursts into applause!

"Nesto!" a fan shouts, and then the audience begins to chant: "Nesto, Nesto, Nesto!"

She doesn't know what to do. She's the center of attention with this bright light upon her. Music starts to play! She sees de la Cruz in the wings, flagging down a guard. "Get her off the stage!" he demands.

The guards hustle onto the stage, scaling the platform to get to her. Meanwhile, Miguel, Hector, Victoria, and Rosita emerge on stage left, opposite de la Cruz. "Sing!" Miguel yells at the moment the guards scramble onto the platform. Mamá Imelda is still in a panic, but then Miguel yells again, "Sing!"

She closes her eyes to concentrate on the music and catch the tune. Then she grasps the mic, holding it close to her mouth. The next part is very difficult, for it goes against every fiber of her being. For years, she has warned against singing, but more important than rules, shoes, and ofrendas is saving her family, especially Miguelito, who needs to go back home.

She begins to sing, her voice quivering from nerves. She's not sure she can pull this off, but then she hears a guitar riff, amplified through the stage speakers. It's a familiar tune Hector used to play.

She takes a deep breath, determined to sing without shaking. Her voice grows stronger, richer.

She spots a guard at the edge of the spotlight, but he stops, confused. She can tell he's afraid to interrupt the show, so she takes advantage. She moves away, the spotlight continually on her, serving as a protective shield against the guards. She starts to descend the staircase at the edge of the platform, and then she sees him: Hector, in the wings, playing his guitar. He smiles, and she smiles back, genuinely happy for his accompaniment.

She continues her song. With every note, she gets more confident. Soon the audience is clapping to the beat, and the stage conductor brings in more instruments, kicking it into high gear.

Mamá Imelda feels herself getting carried away by the music, and as much as she'd like to resist, she just can't. This is too much fun! She doubles down, taking the spotlight with her as she continues to put distance between herself and the guards, trying to reach Miguel so she can give him the photo. One of the guards catches on and tries to block her way. Without missing a beat, Mamá Imelda grabs him and forces him to dance. He freaks out and runs away the first chance he gets. Once the coast is clear, she makes her way across the stage and is about to leave the spotlight when a hand grabs her wrist.

The crowd goes wild! It's Ernesto de la Cruz, and he's harmonizing with her!

He dances Imelda around the stage, all the while trying to get Hector's photo. When she tries to resist, he tightens his grip. When she tries to go offstage, he pivots and pulls her back to the spotlight. When she twirls away from his grasp, he catches her and she falls into a dip. The push and pull of their moves is like a tango. "Let go of me!" she says during a musical interlude, but she can see that de la Cruz is as determined to get the photo as she is to keep it.

The music crescendos. The tempo picks up. It's the finale of the song, and to keep up appearances, de la Cruz guides her into some quick polka steps. That's when Imelda spots an opportunity. At the moment of their highest note, she stomps her heel into his foot, and when he lets go, she runs offstage, photo in hand.

"Ay, ay, ay, ay!" de la Cruz cries—a true grito, born of pain!

The crowd loves it. They cheer, clap, and throw out their own celebratory gritos. But Imelda has no time to bask in the praise. She reaches the wings of the stage and, feeling that adrenaline high, hugs Hector as soon as she sees him. "I forgot what that felt like," she says.

"You . . . you still got it," Hector says, full of admiration.

Then Imelda jumps back to reality and awkwardly pulls

away. She's not ready to completely forgive him, but she's not feeling as angry, either. This time, when he smiles at her, she smiles back.

"Ahem!" comes a voice. It's Miguel.

"Oh!" Imelda says, for they are not there to reminisce about the past. The night is almost over, the sun is rising, and it's time to send the boy home.

She hands him the photo and pulls out her petal. "Miguel," she says, "I give you my blessing." As before, the petal glows. "To go home . . . to put up our photos . . ." She pauses, considering her next words. "And to never—"

"Never play music again," Miguel says with a saddened voice.

Imelda smiles and lifts his chin. She has something else in mind. "To never forget how much your family loves you."

The petal surges, and Miguel's saddened face brightens. She can tell he appreciates these words.

"You're going home," Hector says.

But before Miguel can take the petal and whoosh back to the Land of the Living, de la Cruz barges in. "You're not going anywhere!"

CHAPTER 31

De la Cruz grabs Miguel by the scruff of his hoodie and yanks him away from his great-great-grandparents. Miguel panics. *The man who's always believed in seizing your moment has now literally seized me!* He tries to scramble away, but now that his transformation into a skeleton is nearly complete, he's not as gordo as he used to be. That's why de la Cruz has no trouble dragging him.

Mamá Imelda lunges at de la Cruz, but he pushes her off. Papá Julio and the twin uncles arrive from under the stage, ready for a fight, but de la Cruz warns them away. "Stay back! Stay back!" he says. "All of you!"

That's the last thing Miguel wants, so he pleads with his eyes. His family gets the message. They start closing in on de la Cruz. They will not abandon their child.

"Stay back!" de la Cruz says again. "Not one more step."

The determined family keeps approaching, and with every step they take forward, de la Cruz drags Miguel one step back. Soon they're at a ledge on the very top of the coliseum, near the highest point of the tallest skyscraper in the Land of the Dead. Miguel glances down. It must be a thousand-foot drop to the bottom! Once again, he scrambles with all his might, but de la Cruz is too strong.

"Ernesto, stop!" Hector says, weak and out of breath. "Leave the boy alone."

He stumbles, shimmering like before as he falls. Miguel's heart breaks. This can't be the end! He just met Hector, and after all these years, Hector and Mamá Imelda are finally talking!

"I've worked too hard, Hector," de la Cruz says. "Too hard to let him destroy everything."

With each word, he seems to tighten his grip. The hoodie is pressed hard against Miguel's throat. He reaches for his collar, relieving some of the tension, but not enough to slip free.

Hector pleads. "He's a living child, Ernesto!"

"He's a threat! You think I'd let him go back to the Land of the Living with your photo? To keep your memory alive?" De la Cruz takes a breath and then answers his own question.

"No. Once you're forgotten, no one can discover what I did to you."

"You're a coward!" shouts Miguel. He wants the world to know just how cruel and selfish de la Cruz can be.

"I am Ernesto de la Cruz. The greatest musician of all time!"

"Music is supposed to bring people together," Miguel says. He has never believed it more than now. "You tore my family apart! Hector's the *real* musician. You're just the guy who murdered him and stole his songs!"

De la Cruz ignores him. He's too focused on getting the photo so he can erase what he did—so he can erase Hector, too!

"*I* am the one who is willing to do what it takes to seize my moment," de la Cruz says. Then his voice goes cold and his bony clutch tightens. "Whatever it takes."

He swings Miguel over the ledge, letting the boy hang there.

"Ernesto! No!" Hector begs.

"Apologies, old friend, but the show must go on." He smiles villainously, and then he lets go.

"Ahhh!" Miguel screams, plummeting toward the ground.

"No!" Mamá Imelda's cry rings out from above.

Miguel is in a free fall. The photo flutters in his hand, but he manages to hold on. His legs scramble as if they could climb their way back up, but it's hopeless. They catch nothing but air. The wind whips against his face. "Ahhh!"

he screams again. He's terrified. As he falls, the apartments, shops, and escalators of the giant skyscraper are a blur. He'll hit the bottom soon, and there's nothing he can do to stop!

Then he hears faint howling. He tries to locate the sound, and sure enough, there's Dante, diving toward him with the speed of a lightning bolt!

Dante slices through the sky, grabs Miguel's hoodie, and opens his wings. When they catch the air, Dante and Miguel jerk upward, the sudden movement making Miguel lose his grip on the photo.

"Ahh—no!" Miguel cries as it disappears.

Miguel knows that he will disappear, too, if he and Dante can't escape. They're twisting in the air, struggling to rise. His brave dog has bought him some time, but they are still falling. They are simply too heavy for the small, inexperienced wings. Every time Dante gains a few feet, they lose a few feet more, and the erratic up and down of their flight is loosening Miguel from his hoodie. Before he can adjust, he slides out and once again free-falls!

Panicked, Dante tries to reach him, but he's too slow. Meanwhile, the ground is getting closer and closer. They are nearly beside the pyramids at the base of the skyscraper. Miguel can't believe it's going to end this way after everything he's been through! He closes his eyes and braces for the impact. *One thousand one, one thousand two,* he counts off the seconds. And then . . . *swoosh!*

Instead of hitting the ground, Miguel finds himself on the strong back of a majestic alebrije. It's Pepita! She has swooped in and scooped him up at the last second. And there's Dante, following close behind, wagging his tail and smiling goofily.

Meanwhile, behind the stage curtain, de la Cruz straightens his clothes. They're a bit rumpled from his incident with that meddlesome boy. How could he have ever believed they were related? Then he slicks back his hair and does a few neck rolls to loosen up. At last . . . showtime!

He steps through the curtain. "Ha-ha!" he says as the spotlight beams upon him. Never has he felt more ready to please a crowd.

But they aren't pleased at all. Instead of clapping, they jeer. "Boo! Murderer!"

De la Cruz raises his eyebrows in surprise at their reaction. He tries to play it off. "Please, please, mi familia . . ."

But the audience will not calm down. "Get off the stage!" they shout.

De la Cruz is full of disbelief. Surely they have him confused with someone else. He tries to kick up the orchestra. A little music will clear things up. "Orchestra! The music. A-one, a-two, a-one . . ."

The conductor snaps his baton, and the crowd boos even louder.

Now de la Cruz looks outright mad, like a toro about to charge a matador.

Ignoring the crowd, he grabs the mic. He will seduce them with his most famous song, "Remember Me." A tomato pelts him. "Hey!" The next thing he knows, a few spit wads ping his face, and then a smorgasbord of kiwis, coconuts, bananas, corncobs, melons, and blueberries splatters and leaves a wet gooey mess on his designer clothes.

"Look!" someone shouts.

All eyes gaze at the space behind him. He turns, and on the stadium screens he sees a giant jaguar alebrije rising above the upper ledge of the coliseum with . . . no, it can't be . . . with Miguel on her back! She lands backstage. The boy slides off and runs into the waiting arms of his family.

"He's all right!" someone from the crowd exclaims.

"He didn't fall to the ground!"

"He narrowly escaped death at the hands of that imposter!"

De la Cruz suddenly understands the jeers of the crowd. All his backstage treachery was projected to the Land of the Dead. Someone had turned on the cameras and microphones! Someone had broadcast the image of him holding Miguel hostage and letting him go where he was sure to die! Someone had let the whole world hear de la Cruz admit that he would do anything—even murder!—to get what he wants.

"What? How?!" he mutters as he tries to figure out who the traitor was, for surely it was someone in the stage crew.

How will he ever spin this? It's a PR nightmare!

He glances back at the screens, and to his horror, the image of Pepita grows larger and larger. She is prowling past the camera and then . . .

She pokes her head through the curtain and locks eyes

on him! He stumbles back a few steps. Her penetrating gaze makes him feel like a helpless lizard about to be caught beneath powerful feline claws.

"Nice kitty!" he tries.

Pepita roars. Then she lifts into the sky, grabbing de la Cruz with her talons and flinging him through the air like a kitten playing with a ball of yarn.

"Ahhh!" he cries. "Put me down! No, please! I beg of you, stop! Stop! No!"

His screaming only encourages her. She tosses him, catches him, and tosses him again, each throw making him yelp with fear. Then she swings him around and around, and when she has enough momentum, she hurls him out of the coliseum.

"No! Aaahhh!" he cries.

As he flies past, the crowd points and shouts, "Murderer! Murderer!" And when he slams into a giant church bell, they erupt into applause!

CHAPTER 32

Miguel has never been so happy to see his family. He can't thank them enough for defending him. Papá Julio, the uncles, Hector, Mamá Imelda—they did their best against the guards.

Tía Rosita and Tía Victoria come running from a back corridor. "Did you see what we did?" Before the family can answer, Tía Rosita explains. "We filmed the whole thing and broadcast it live."

"No one will ever trust or praise de la Cruz again," Tía Victoria says.

"But how?" Mamá Imelda asks. "Since when do you know how to work stage equipment?"

They chuckle. "We had a little practice," Tía Rosita says, "when we were searching for Miguel earlier."

"So the whole world knows the truth?" Miguel asks. When his aunts nod, he turns to share the good news with Hector, who's sitting against the wall, exhausted. "Did you hear tha—"

He stops mid-sentence. Hector is struggling to stand, so Miguel runs to support him. "Hector!" he says, the events of his free fall flooding back. "The photo, I lost it."

"It's okay, m'ijo. It's—" Suddenly, Hector suffers his most violent flickering yet, and once again, he collapses.

Miguel kneels beside him. "Hector! Hector!"

The frail man can barely move his limbs. "My Coco . . ." Hector says, his voice fading.

"No!" Miguel cries. "We can still find the photo."

At that moment, a beam of sunlight peeks over the horizon. Miguel feels its warmth on his cheek. He knows what this means. He has to make a choice—save Hector or save himself.

"Miguel," Mamá Imelda says, "it's almost sunrise."

"No, no, no, I can't leave you!" He turns to Hector. "I promised I'd put your photo up. I promised you'd see Coco!"

Hector looks at Miguel, and in the glassy reflection of his great-great-grandfather's eyes, Miguel can see the skeletal transformation creeping onto the edges of his face.

The shimmering of Hector's bones advances. "We're both out of time, m'ijo."

"No, no! She can't forget you!" Miguel feels overwhelmed with guilt. If only he'd held on tighter to the photo, to his whole family! He glances at the circle of loved ones. There are tears in their eyes, but he can see that they all agree—Miguel must go home.

"I just wanted her to know that I loved her," Hector says.

He musters all his strength to grab a marigold petal.

"Hector." Miguel's sobbing now. He doesn't want to become a skeleton, but he doesn't want to leave, either. He just met his ancestors. Why can't they have more time?

"You have our blessing," Hector says.

"No conditions," adds Mamá Imelda.

The petal glows. Hector struggles to lift the petal to Miguel. He's too weak, so Mamá Imelda takes his hand in hers.

"No, Papá Hector. Please!"

Imelda and Hector move their joined hands toward Miguel's chest. Hector fades even more, his eyelids begin to close, and he utters one last wish. "Go home . . ."

"I promise!" Miguel cries out with determination. "I won't let Coco forget—"

Whoosh! Once again, a whirlwind of marigold petals carries Miguel away, and everything goes white.

A few seconds later, Miguel finds himself back in de la Cruz's tomb. The first thing he does is glance at his hands.

They're no longer skeletal! They've got skin and muscle and everything. He pokes his face. It's squishy with flesh again! Sunlight filters through the window. It's morning now.

He spots the skull guitar on the floor, the guitar that made Ernesto de la Cruz famous—Papá Hector's guitar! For a moment Miguel is outraged, but then he remembers that Hector didn't care about fame. He cared only about family. "Maybe it's not too late," he mutters to himself as he picks up the guitar. "Maybe it's not too late!" he shouts, his voice echoing in the tomb.

He sprints out of the cemetery, guitar in hand. He races through the plaza, past the statue of de la Cruz. He runs through the streets of Santa Cecilia, kicking up dirt as he speeds by.

When he gets to the hacienda, Tío Berto and Primo Abel are sleeping on a bench. Miguel blows right past them, and they jolt awake. Abel falls off. Tío Berto calls out, "There he is!"

Papá spots him. "Miguel?! Stop!" But Miguel's in a hurry. No time to explain.

He rounds the corner and follows the trail of marigold petals through the front gate. He runs for the back bedroom, but just as he gets to the doorway, Abuelita steps up and blocks him. He skids to a stop, nearly crashing into her. "Ah!"

"Where have you been?!"

"I need to see Mamá Coco," he says, and then, respectfully, "Please."

But all Abuelita can see is the guitar. "What are you doing with that?! Give it to me!"

Miguel hates to defy her, but he has urgent business. Besides, he has Mamá Imelda's blessing, and if *she* can learn to love music again, then maybe . . . maybe . . .

Without another moment of hesitation, he pushes past Abuelita and slams the door shut behind him.

"Miguel! Stop! Miguel! Miguel! Miguel!"

He locks the door and takes a deep breath. He'll have to explain later, but not right now. He's running out of time. *Hector's* running out of time, and Miguel *has* to keep his promise.

He faces the room, the morning sun brightening the space. Mamá Coco's in her wicker wheelchair, but even with all the commotion, she doesn't seem to notice that he's there. Miguel hopes he's not too late.

"Mamá Coco? Can you hear me? It's Miguel." He looks into her eyes, but all he gets back is a vacant stare. "I saw your papá," he says. "Remember? Papá? Please—if you forget him, he'll be gone . . . forever!"

She doesn't respond, not even when Miguel's father starts banging on the door.

"Miguel, open this door!" he orders.

But Miguel's too focused on his promise. He shows Mamá Coco the guitar. "Here," he says. "This was his guitar, right? He used to play it to you? See, there he is." He shows her the picture with the faceless musician.

Nothing. Her eyes are glass.

Miguel tries again. "Papá, remember? Papá?"

Mamá Coco continues to stare blankly, as if he isn't there.

"Miguel!" his father calls angrily.

"Mamá Coco, please. Please don't forget him."

Suddenly, he hears keys rattling at the door. He tugs at Mamá Coco's shawl, begging her to remember. Then the door flies open and the entire family pours in.

"What are you doing to that poor woman?" Abuelita asks as she brushes him aside to comfort Mamá Coco. "It's okay, Mamita. It's okay."

"What's gotten into you?" Papá scolds.

Miguel sinks from the weight of his failure. He looks down, defeated, and tears drip off his nose. Back in the Land of the Dead, Hector came through for him, but Miguel has let his great-great-grandfather down. All he wanted was to give Hector the thing he wanted most—to let Mamá Coco know he loved her.

He's beside himself with grief when he feels a warm hand on his shoulder. It's Papá, pulling Miguel into an embrace. "I thought I'd lost you."

"I'm sorry, Papá," Miguel sobs.

Then Mamá steps forward. "We're all together now. That's what matters." She puts her arms around him, too. Miguel is happy to be reunited with his parents, but he can't help thinking that his family is still not whole.

"It's okay, Mamita," Abuelita says to her mother as she

pats the older woman's arm. Then she turns to Miguel. "You apologize to your mamá Coco!"

Miguel sniffles, and then he goes to her. "Mamá Coco . . ." He's about to apologize when the little scraggly cat jumps onto the windowsill. Miguel does a double take, for something in the way the cat lands reminds him of Pepita. Then he sees Hector's skull guitar.

"Well?" Abuelita demands, arms crossed. "Apologize!"

But Miguel has another idea. "Mamá Coco? Your papá— he wanted you to have this." He picks up the guitar. Abuelita reaches for it, but Papá takes her arm. "Mamá," he says, "wait."

Then Miguel starts to sing "Remember Me"—not the flashy version made famous by Ernesto de la Cruz, but Hector's version, almost a lullaby and full of love. As he sings it, he pictures Papá Hector, Mamá Imelda, and all of his relatives—in the Land of the Dead and the Land of the Living.

He almost doesn't notice when his mother gasps.

"Look," Mamá says, pointing to Mamá Coco. The vacant stare is gone. There's a glimmer in the old woman's eyes, and they grow brighter with every note. Her cheeks soften and get plump. Her lips arc into a smile. It's as if she's being fed by the memories of her father.

Encouraged, Miguel continues to sing. He pours all his love into the song, uttering notes as gentle as marigold petals against the cheek.

Mamá Coco's brows lift, delighted, and the family can

only gape, dumbfounded by this sign of awareness and life. Then, brimming with joy, Mamá Coco joins Miguel and sings along! Her voice, scratchy with age, and his, clear with youth, somehow come together in beautiful harmony. They sing about remembering a special someone—about remembering Hector.

Tears stream down Abuelita's face as she watches. The music—and its effect on Mamá Coco—has softened her heart, and all her anger has gone away. There is only love on her face. It's as if she's witnessed a miracle.

"Elena?" Mamá Coco says, noticing her daughter's tears. "What's wrong, m'ija?"

Abuelita wipes her eyes. "Nothing, Mamá. Nothing at all."

Mamá Coco turns to Miguel. "My papá used to sing me that song."

"He loved you," Miguel says, finally fulfilling Hector's wish. "Your papá loved you so much."

She smiles, and Miguel can tell she has waited a long time to hear those words. Then she turns to her nightstand and, with a shaky hand, opens a drawer and pulls out a notebook. Mamá Coco peels back the lining of the book to reveal a scrap of paper. She hands it to Miguel, and . . .

It's the missing face from the photo—*Hector!*

Miguel pieces the picture together, seeing Hector as he was in life—a handsome young man with a happy smile. Thanks to Mamá Coco, Miguel will get to keep his entire promise, for the next time this photo goes on the ofrenda, it will have Hector's face!

"Thank you," Mamá Coco tells Miguel, "for helping me remember." Then she turns to the family. "Papá was a musician. When I was a little girl, he and Mamá would sing such beautiful songs. . . ."

She continues with her stories and the entire family gathers around to listen. Miguel can only guess what's happening in the Land of the Dead, but he feels confident that Mamá Coco's memories are giving Hector strength, and instead of dusty and gray, his bones are gleaming white!

CHAPTER 33

The following year, Santa Cecilia once again prepares for Día de los Muertos. Vendors in the market sell marigolds, pan dulce, alebrijes, and sugar skulls—everything except Ernesto de la Cruz souvenirs.

In Mariachi Plaza, ballet folklórico dancers warm up for a performance, this time with shoes made by the famous Rivera family, and musicians register for the annual talent show, noting a new performer on the list—a boy named Miguel.

Visitors to the cemetery dust and polish headstones and leave behind offerings as they share stories about their departed loved ones. Nearly every gravesite is attended, but one lies neglected—the tomb of Ernesto de la Cruz. Someone has hung a sign that says *Forget you* around his statue, and that's exactly what's happening.

Even the tour guide has forgotten him. This year, he rushes right past the once-famous statue in Mariachi Plaza, and instead, stops in front of the Rivera Shoes Workshop. "And right here," he informs the tourists, "is one of Santa Cecilia's greatest treasures . . . the home of the esteemed songwriter Hector Rivera." The crowd snaps pictures of the famous skull guitar and framed letters to Coco. "The letters Hector wrote home for his daughter, Coco, contain the lyrics for all of your favorite songs, not just 'Remember Me.'"

Sometimes the tour guide requests an appearance from one of the Riveras, but today they are too busy with their own preparations. Prima Rosa and Primo Abel decorate the hacienda with papel picado. Papá Franco sweeps the courtyard. The young twins, Manny and Benny, sprinkle petals to create a marigold path, while Papá and Mamá work on tamales.

And this time, instead of sneaking away, Miguel joins Abuelita in the ofrenda room.

"And that man is your papá Julio," Miguel tells his baby sister, Socorro. She's named after her great-grandmother, who went by the nickname Coco. Abuelita arranges the photos as Miguel holds his sister and points out their relatives. "And there's Tía Rosita, and Tía Victoria, and those two are Oscar and Felipe." He shares a few stories from his adventures in the Land of the Dead, laughing at some of their antics. "These aren't just old pictures," he says. "They're our family, and they're counting on us to remember them."

Abuelita smiles to see her grandson passing on the tradition. Then she places a new picture on the ofrenda, a photo of Mamá Coco. She passed away a few months ago, but not before sharing her memories of Hector and of how she once secretly danced. After learning this, Miguel realized that the discarded shoes in the hideout belonged to her. He spent several weeks repairing and cleaning them so they looked brand-new. He still prefers music, but fixing Mamá Coco's shoes has given him a new appreciation for the family trade. He felt proud as he left them at her grave, and he smiles now as he imagines Mamá Coco seeing the offering and wearing her dance shoes once again.

When he spots a tear on Abuelita's cheek, he puts an arm around her.

"I miss her," she says.

"Me too."

After a few moments, Abuelita recovers and makes a few more adjustments. "How's that?" she asks.

"Perfect," Miguel answers, and it *is* perfect, because right next to Mamá Coco's picture is the photo of Mamá Imelda, baby Coco, and Papá Hector, his face taped in place, the family finally restored.

Meanwhile, at Marigold Grand Central Station, Hector anxiously waits in line. He isn't hiding in a raspa cart. He isn't dressed as Frida Kahlo. He hasn't painted alebrije patterns on his bones. He is simply himself, only this time, he has new clothes and a new pair of boots made by the loving hands of his wife, Imelda. They fit perfectly and, Hector marvels, "They don't give me blisters."

"Enjoy your visit," the departures agent says to the couple in front of Hector. And then, "Next!"

Hector takes a deep breath and steps up. When the agent recognizes him, Hector shrugs and chuckles nervously. Then the monitor scans him, and instead of buzzing, it dings! For the first time in his afterlife, he has been approved!

The agent smiles. "Enjoy your visit, Hector!"

Hector tips his hat, and his chest swells as he approaches the Marigold Bridge. He can't help glancing back and feeling pleasantly surprised to find no one chasing him.

Mamá Imelda waits at the foot of the bridge, and she kisses him when he joins her. Then he hears, "Papá!" It's Coco, running toward them. Hector gives her a giant hug, because each moment with Coco is a miracle.

As the family steps onto the bridge, the petals glow. Hector can't help singing, Coco can't help dancing, and Mamá Imelda can't help adding a few cumbia steps and her own voice to the song.

The sun has finally set in Santa Cecilia. Once again, fireworks light the sky, and their colorful glow reveals a shadow on the courtyard wall—a little alebrije with small wings and a flapping tongue. When it turns a corner, it's just a normal Xolo dog, Dante. Then another shadow looms large—a jaguar with giant wings—Pepita! But when *she* turns the corner, the shadow shrinks to fit the scraggly alley cat that has watched over the family all these years.

"Roo! Roo!" Dante calls as he joins the family in the courtyard. Pepita follows, weaving among the family's legs.

Instead of shooing them away, Abuelita tosses the animals tamales. Then she offers servings to the rest of the family, kissing Papá Franco on the cheek when he grabs his share.

In the center of the courtyard, Miguel plays a guitar and sings, but he is not alone—for Mamá Coco has made her way there, too, beaming with pride that Miguel has returned music to the family. Primo Abel shakes a tambourine and Prima Rosa blows into a harmonica. The rest of the Riveras—both the living and the dead—join the chorus. Tías Rosita and Victoria sway their hips. Tíos Oscar and Felipe copy each of Benny and Manny's moves. Mamá Imelda admires the new baby in Mamá's arms. Mamá Coco and Papá Julio place their hands on Abuelita's shoulder. And Hector shows off his dance moves, using his skull as a drum, twirling his tibia, and strumming his ribcage.

Aunts, uncles, cousins, parents, children—living and dead—all wearing comfortable shoes and all celebrating. Music has *not* torn them apart after all. Instead, it's the very thing that has brought them together.

Rivera

Tío Felipe   Tío Oscar

Tía Rosita   Papá Julio

Tía Victoria

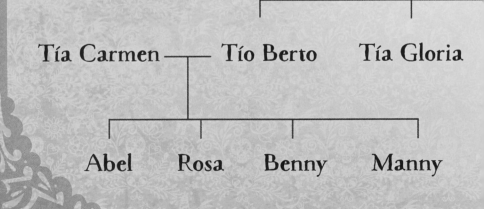

Tía Carmen —— Tío Berto   Tía Gloria

Abel   Rosa   Benny   Manny

FAMILY TREE

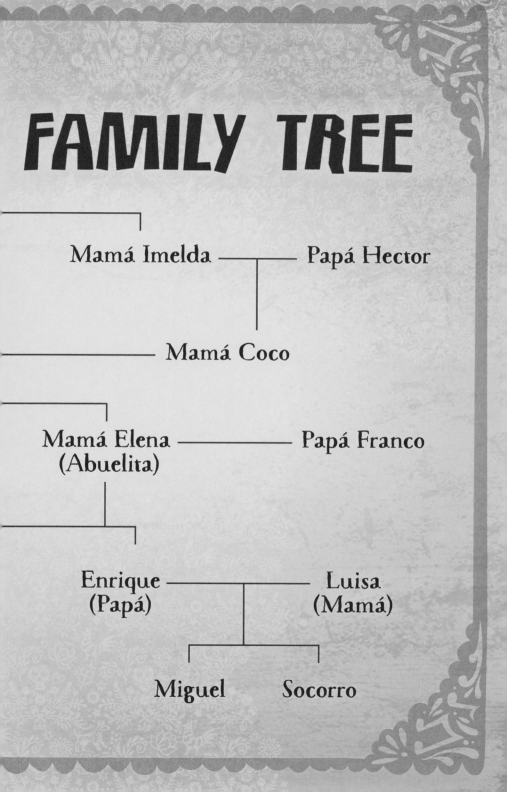

Mamá Imelda ——— Papá Hector

Mamá Coco

Mamá Elena ——— Papá Franco
(Abuelita)

Enrique ——— Luisa
(Papá)   (Mamá)

Miguel   Socorro

Diana López is the author of award-winning middle grade novels, *Confetti Girl, Ask My Mood Ring How I Feel,* and *Nothing Up My Sleeve.* Her latest book is *Lucky Luna.* Visit her at www.dianalopezbooks.com.